From Böd to Boardroom

From Böd to Boardroom

**An historical novel
on the life of Arthur Anderson**

D. Hilda Peterson

The Shetland Times Ltd.,
Lerwick.
2001

From Böd to Boardroom
An historical novel on the life of Arthur Anderson

ISBN 1 898852 79 0

First published by The Shetland Times Ltd., 2001.

British Library Cataloguing-in-Publication Data
A catalogue record for this book is available from the British Library.

Printed and published by
The Shetland Times Ltd.,
Prince Alfred Street, Lerwick,
Shetland, Scotland.
ZE1 0EP, UK.

To my sisters: Rona, Sylvia and Ireen.

Contents

Foreword

Hilda Peterson's latest book covers the life of Arthur Anderson. A Shetlander, he rose from humble beginnings at Lerwick, where his father was in charge of a fish curing beach at Gremista, to become a prominent businessman, and, as co-founder of the P&O shipping company, a pioneer of transport by steamship.

The country was at war with France when Arthur joined the Royal Navy. His opportunity came when he arrived at Portsmouth to join the crew of the 94-gun *Ardent*, which was on her way to the Baltic.

He started a new career in 1815 when he became clerk to a London businessman, Brodie Willcox. By 1822 they were in partnership as ship charterers. The company established strong links with Portugal and was involved in gun-running to help restore the Queen of Portugal to her throne, a service which she never forgot and which no doubt played a part in the company's success in winning the contract to run a mail service to Spain and Portugal by steamship.

Their success in this part of Europe was a major factor in their winning the contract to operate a shipping service to the Far East and the establishment of the Peninsular and Oriental Steam Navigation Company, better known today as P&O.

This historical novel demonstrates Arthur Anderson's devotion to his native islands. He promoted the sale of Shetland knitwear in London; he tried to improve the conditions of Shetland fishermen with an experimental fish-curing venture on the island of Vaila; he founded Shetland's first newspaper *The Shetland Journal*, which campaigned against some of the worst abuses of that time. Mindful of the heavy loss of life at sea, he provided funds for the building of the Widows Homes at Lerwick. Mindful too of his own struggle to acquire a basic education he paid for the building of what was then the Anderson Educational Institute.

Throughout this book there are marvellous reconstructions of life in Lerwick as Arthur Anderson would have remembered it – the unsavoury appearance of the town, the hardships and the almost total lack of education unless paid for.

From time to time bits of local history come alive in this book – like the tragedy on Tingwall loch involving the family of the minister, Rev John Turnbull. Or the tale of Kirstie Caddel, who, evicted from her home with her children, died on the cold stairhead of Lerwick's Town House.

Changes had to come and in the forefront of these was Arthur Anderson.

His opportunity to fight for his native islands came when he was elected as their Member of Parliament.

James R. Nicolson.

Acknowledgments

I am much indebted to James R. Nicolson for taking time to review this book and for writing the foreword.

Sons and Daughters of Shetland proved to be a mine of information on many of the characters mentioned in the story.

John Nicolson's biography of Arthur Anderson gave valuable insight into Arthur's life and accomplishments.

My grateful thanks to the secretary of Lord Sterling, P&O Group Chairman, for confirming the accuracy of Arthur Anderson's P&O background and for best wishes for the success of this novel.

Many thanks to Mrs Elizabeth Laurenson, Lerwick, for typing the manuscript.

Chapter 1

Young Arthur

A rthur Anderson woke to the early morning sun shining through the little attic window of Da Böd of Gremista. Rubbing his eyes, he tried to stretch his legs in the box bed but it was too short. Jumping out onto the tatted mat he did some exercises then, exchanging his long nightshirt for trousers and jumper, he rushed downstairs.

Collecting two wooden buckets from the but room Arthur opened the front door and set off to the well for water. He breathed in the lovely fresh air of a Shetland morning. Several gulls were quarrelling over scraps of fish left on the beach from the previous day and a lark flew from the ground nearby, singing as it rose into the sky. Otherwise, all was quiet. A cock crowed but Arthur's mind was already too full of the jobs that would occupy his day to notice.

Arriving at the well he removed a large stone and dipped his buckets to fill them. Taking one in each hand he made for the house again. His mother met him at the door and helped him to put the buckets on a shelf. Elizabeth Anderson took a mug and filled a pot with water then hung the pot on a chain hanging from the chimney.

"Will you fetch me some peats from the stack?" she asked.

"Yae Midder," answered the boy and he picked up a basket from beside the fire his mother had just set up with peats. It had been 'rested' the night before by clearing the hot ashes to the side of the open chimney hearth. Small, live peats were taken from the ashes and placed on the heart again with new ones nosed into them. Another row of peats was laid out on the heart to warm for beginning the fire again in the morning.

"Well, son," said Robert Anderson, "you are always up early finding something to do to help."

"I must do my chores before I go into Lerwick today," the boy answered. "I've got Bess ready to take to the hill for more peats."

Arthur put a saddle on the small Shetland pony and attached mesh panniers to each side. He led the pony up the well-trodden path behind the house to the hill beyond where the peats had been cut from the hillside. Every now and then Bess would stop for a nibble of fresh green grass and the boy would take a breather.

When they reached the peat-bank Arthur filled the two panniers with peats then sat down for a rest on the heather-clad turf. As he looked towards Bressay he noted how the island made a wonderful back-drop to the harbour of Bressay Sound where many boats were sheltering, some small Dutch vessels with rowing boats plying between them and the shore, one or two sailing boats and one particularly large three-masted ship.

"I would love to go on one of those," said the boy to himself – his imagination running away with him. He could see himself climbing aloft and out on the yards to unfurl or reef the massive sails, especially on a windy day! A nudge on his shoulder from Bess startled the boy and he rose quickly from his reverie.

"Come on Bess, hurry. I see a navy cutter in, they'll be coming to get the men for their ship."

Sitting in to breakfast, Arthur told his parents what he had seen in the harbour.

"I am expecting a number of boats today," Robert Anderson said to his wife, "the fishing station is doing well at the moment. I'm glad Sir Arthur Nicolson saw fit to put me in charge of his station here in Gremista. He is a fine man and I enjoyed working for him in North Roe. It was fortunate this booth was ready when we needed it."

Sir Arthur had employed John Murray, his joiner from the south, to come up and plenish the house. He made a good job of the box-beds and wooden staircase and also all the chairs, tables and other furnishings. Luckily Sir Arthur could afford to do that and it suited Anderson's purpose well.

Da Böd was so much bigger than the small cottage Robert and Elizabeth had stayed in at North Roe. There was a living room on the ground floor to the left of the front door which was used at all times for cooking meals, knitting, spinning, 'kirnin' the milk to make butter, mending nets and farm implements and talking to visitors over a cup of tea. To the right of the front door was a larger room used as a store with its door on the north gable. There were huge vats for salting the fish, lines and hooks, lamps and most things necessary for the fishing boats. On the first floor was a bedroom, closet and the 'best room' where important visitors were entertained and on the second floor were two smaller rooms used as bedrooms.

As Robert and his wife had toured the house when they moved in it appeared like a castle to them.

"This will be a wonderful place to bring up a family," said Elizabeth as they came down the stairs together.

"Yes," answered Robert, "if the Lord will and we are spared."

"They say it's to be a dry summer again," mused Robert, "so I expect we'll have people coming to our well for water. The other day as I passed Mounthooly Street there were surely forty folks waiting their turn to get a bucketful, but ours never runs dry. I believe one man takes barrels to Bressay and fills them there then rows back to Lerwick and sells the water. We are very fortunate here to have our own well – and one which never runs dry at that!"

"Many folks have to walk miles to get to their peat-banks but ours is situated just up the hill from the house so could not be better. We'll get a good sized stack of peats if it's going to be dry weather. It also makes working them a lot easier as they can be handled quicker when they are dry. It helps with the hay too to get the grass cut and cured then built into the stack when it's fine weather and it's the same with the corn. So much depends on the dry days."

Elizabeth poured porridge from a pot into bowls, set them on the table then put eggs on to boil. She poured milk from a larger bowl into a jug after skimming the cream from the top. It was delicious with the 'gruel'. There were slices of bacon from the pig that had been killed in the winter and 'bannocks' baked on the grid-iron at the open fire the day before.

"So you are off to Lerwick today to see Mr Turnbull," Robert said to his son, "I will come with you. He is only teaching till he gets an appointment as minister in one of the country districts. You will not have to speak in dialect at school and always address your tutor as 'Master'. It is a great pity there are no schools in the islands. I know Thomas Gifford of Busta has tried for many years to introduce them but they will come in time. Now, if you are ready, we will go."

"Wait you," said Elizabeth, "I have your lunch ready Arthur. There's bannocks in the bag and milk in the mug. Don't lose it now. That's the horn mug that 'Auld Da' had at the fishing with him. Blessings be with you."

As the man and boy walked away from the house Elizabeth wiped a tear from her eye with the corner of her apron. "Peerie soul," she whispered to herself.

Arthur turned quickly at the corner of the house and rushed back and gave his mother a hug. "Thanks Mother," he said and ran after his father.

Women coming to the doors of their cottages would pass the time of day with 'Mester Anderson'.

"See you, he's taking the peerie boy to school," said one. "Yes," said her neighbour, "and a lot of good it'll do him." "He'd be far better working with his hands," said another. "No," observed the first woman," a bit a 'lair' or learning never hurt anyone."

Looking up the Staney Hill they saw crofters cutting their peats while others were digging the small fields behind their cottages. Shawls were pegged out on the grass to dry, while socks and gloves hung on boards in the sunshine along with fish on lines.

"A wonderful day," said Robert as he passed an old lady with a basket of peats on her back. "Any word of Mansie since he went to sea?" he asked.

"Yes, we get two or three lines now and again. He's doing fine. He's not scrubbing decks now! He's been promoted to second mate." So saying the old woman trudged on with her burden, knitting all the while.

The gutters huts were noisy as they passed, with the voices of the women getting ready for gutting and sorting the herring. Each helped the other to bandage their fingers to save them being cut from the sharp knives used to gut the fish. They were a cheery lot with their bright scarves around their heads and striped skirts and aprons.

As they passed the curing station, alive with industry, Arthur asked his father why there were so many barrels stacked about. Above the noise of the coopers hammering metal hoops which went round 'staves' to form barrels, Robert told his son that boats came from many countries to buy the herrings which were in plentiful supply around the shores of Shetland. It was mainly the Dutch who bought them and took them back to Holland. The barrels were put on the smaller boats which delivered them to larger ones going back to their country. The fish were placed in the barrels then a layer of salt added then fish and salt time about till the barrel was filled.

"Ah! Here is Francis Yates. I believe he was the first cooper to work in Shetland," Robert told his son.

"How are things today?" asked Robert.

"Very busy sir. There are plenty of herring this year. It's hard work making the barrels though. The staves are put in place then the iron bands round the barrels have to be hammered into shape," Francis explained to the boy. He turned to Robert. "Did I ever tell you the story about Freddie the fiddler? His son, Andrew was, like his father, very keen on music, but he had no money to buy a fiddle, or violin as they call them, so he got the stave of a barrel and put a string on it then got someone to tune it for him! When Andrew went to the whaling at Greenland he was presented with a new fiddle!" He went on his way chuckling to himself.

"I would love to sail in one of those ships" said Arthur looking wistfully at a large sailing boat as it entered the sound.

"All in good time," said his father.

"Here's the mount with the fort. This is where the soldiers stay. James Malcolmson is Captain Commander of the Fort just now. They say there are two hundred men here. The barrack master is John Mouat. He has just finished building Annsbrae House and these foundations at the top of Charlotte Lane are to be a house eventually. We'll have to climb this hill to the back of the mount and go along the Sound scattald a bit then down by the Garrison Close to the shore."

Passing the scattald, they saw men bundling up calf hides to to ship away for sale. There were a number of cattle and sheep which some crofters were selling and buying. Sheep fleeces were sorted too and set aside to sell.

"We'll go through the gate and past Jeannie Gordon's cottage. She still has a thatched roof. There are not many of them left now."

"There's a lot of houses here," the boy pointed out as they walked along the shore to their left. "Who stays in that one with the high walls?"

"That's where James Keldray stays. You've heard about the smugglers? James told them to put some barrels ashore at a passage beneath his house. His wife was pretty smart so she emptied the barrels and hid the brandy. Next day when the men came for their money Keldray said that the barrels were empty and would not pay for the spirits. The smugglers were furious. When Keldray went to open his door next day he found an effigy of himself hanging from a rope!"

The pair walked on in silence till Robert pointed to an old building which he said was a trading booth.

"Watch your feet," he shouted. "This is the Heddels burn and it's pretty full today. There's a good bit of sea on and it's coming up to the 'trance'. Wait you, we'll be able to jump over the burn here and then go up Mounthooly Closs."

"Here comes James Ritchie, he is the tidemaster in the customs. He usually puts a notice up in the window to tell when the tides are full or ebbing so the sailors can judge what is the correct time to sail."

"Well James, it's a full tide today, the sea is right up to the trance."

"Yes sir, the moon is full just now."

"Father, here comes peerie Gibbie the bellman. What is he shouting?"

"He says that John Innes, the surgeon, is performing operations today and if anyone wants their garden done they are to get in touch with Alex Ramsay".

"What a smell," said Arthur, "can they not clean the place of all this rubbish lying around?"

"They would need to," answered Robert, "our beach at Gremista is kept so fine and clean for the fish to dry on."

"Why are all these folks gathered here?" asked Arthur as they climbed Mounthooly Closs. "That's their well and they have come for water," was the reply.

"What? All these people get their water from one well? I'm glad we have our own well" said Arthur as he hurried by.

"We are very fortunate," added his father, "I believe this place is a den of iniquity in the evenings. Drunk folks about in the daytime and fights going on all the time. We are better off where we are."

"Is it far now father?"

"Not long now, in fact we are right there. Here is Mr Turnbull himself. Good-day, to you sir," greeted Robert.

"Good day to you too," replied the tutor, "and this is the young man hoping to join us today?" He put an arm around the boy's shoulder and guided him on to the house.

Robert would miss his son helping him at the station as he would never get another boy so conscientious to work for him. Walking back down the hill Robert came to the beach and turning southwards passed Norna's Court where Barbara Pitcairn had lived at her father's house after being sent from Busta by the Giffords where she had had a boy to the eldest son, John. He and his three brothers were drowned when their boat overturned as they were crossing from Wethersta. The couple were secretly married but the Giffords would not believe it.

Barbara was not accepted in the house by Mrs Gifford and was sent to Lerwick in 1756 when her son was seven years old. He only saw his mother once after that on his way to college in Aberdeen. Barbara died shortly afterwards.

Several boats were ebbed-up on Sinclair's Beach. Above the banks were North Kirk and South Kirk Closses and beyond, the Bullister peat banks. Passing the half-Nepkin, Robert noticed boats tied up at the Cockstool Rock, rocking in the waves. He wondered if Thomas Bolt of Cruister had crossed the sound from Bressay as he was on his way to see him on business. Arriving at Lochend House he was told that Mr Bolt had not yet come in so carried on walking south past Leog House and eventually came to Twageos House where Elizabeth's friend, Margaret Henry, worked for the Chalmers family.

Remembering he had to order new tongs for the peat fire, he went into Andrew Erasmusson's, the blacksmiths at Leog.

"Good day Andrew. I wonder if I could order a pair of taings for the fire. When would they be ready do you think?"

"In a week's time," was the reply.

As Robert emerged from the smiddy he looked towards Bressay and saw a large cod boat dredging up mussels for fishing bait. He scowled. Nearing the steps below Lochend House he saw Bolt's boat approaching.

"Glad to see you safe," shouted Robert as Thomas Bolt hurried up the steps.

"Where is young Arthur today? You were to bring him with you."

"He has gone to Mr Turnbull's school. He seems anxious to learn."

Arriving in the house, Thomas poured a dram for them both.

"I see one of those cod boats dredging up mussels for bait off the South Ness," said Robert. "They take them up wholesale then throw away the small ones clinging to them and dump them ashore. When we lift them we throw back the smaller shells into the sea to spawn and grown again. The 'scaaps' will soon be bare and we need the mussels for our own handlines."

"That's true," said Thomas Bolt as he thought on what his friend had said. "The tusk and bigger fish can be caught with fish bait. If all the mussels go what bait can we get for catching the haddock?"

"It will likely take years to stop these sloops taking the bait but we will have to speak to the higher authorities about it."

"Yes," said Thomas thoughtfully, "it's a sad day when we see our bait taken away. I got your order for new materials to be sent to the station. I'll see they are delivered right away."

"Splendid," said Robert rising to leave, "good-day."

Instead of retracing his steps along the shore Robert turned up the 'Dra Well' lane and came out near Gracie Mulla's thatched cottage and made his way to Annsbrae and along the head of the hill on the road towards the mount. It was a fine road to walk on and his thoughts reverted to the time when Holland was at war and soldiers were stationed in the town; they built the road for easy access from the fort, where they were garrisoned, to the Knab where they had a defence lookout over the south entrance to Bressay Sound.

It seemed a long walk back to Gremista without his son but Robert was soon back home.

"How did you get on?" asked Elizabeth anxiously.

"Fine," answered Robert feeling a lump in his throat. "On a fine day like this the boy should have been out in the sunshine enjoying the fresh air and not cooped up in a hot house. Still, there will be other good days before winter sets in."

"I've made tea," said his wife as she busied herself to keep her mind occupied, "and some bannocks." A tear fell on her hand which she quickly wiped away, "and to think that our eldest has gone to school already," she whispered.

Robert rose from his chair and put a comforting arm around his wife. "Never you fear for him, he'll go far."

Chapter 2

Disappointment

Elizabeth put on her best shawl and walked the mile and a half north to Vatsland where her friend lived. Anne Gray was a seamstress and Elizabeth was going to order a new frock for her daughter. She took a small basket of fresh-baked bannocks and butter with her. She enjoyed the walk as it was a beautiful day. She was careful to note the many wild flowers growing at the side of the path, some with deep colours, others delicate. She and Robert often walked to the point of Kebister Ness beyond Vatsland.

When she arrived at the cottage, she knocked and went in. "How are you today?" she asked.

"Very well," answered Anne rising from the table. "What can I do for you today?"

"I would like you to make a 'shepherdess' frock for Barbara. She has outgrown the last one you made but was very fond of the design, long with frilled edges and puffed sleeves."

"What colours would she like this time?"

"Maybe a pretty velvet, green with a white collar."

"Will you take a cup of tea while you are here?" asked Anne, hoping her visitor would stay as she was often lonely – her house being so far from the town or other cottages.

"Thank you, yes, I would enjoy that. These are a few things I baked today. I always remember how good you were to the children when I was ill, looking after them every day until I was better. You have a way with children – they are all very fond of you."

"That was a pleasure," said Anne, "it was fine to do something for you for a change, you are so good helping others yourself."

As Elizabeth rose to go, she thanked her hostess for the tea and said she would call again to see if the dress was ready.

As Elizabeth approached Da Böd, she realised how fortunate her family was to be living at Gremista. She had been brought up at the 'Ness' 20 miles south of Lerwick.

She loved the freedom of the country and open spaces, the fresh air and the quiet that descended in the evenings when the noisy sound of work was done. She thought of the description of the town Robert had mentioned when he got home that morning. He had seemed reluctant to take the boy to town and now she knew why. The town was in a terrible condition, middens in the lanes and rubbish thrown in every corner. The wells were overcrowded with queues waiting their turn for water. Who knew what hovel the person drawing water from the well before you had come from? Even in the day-time drunk people crossed one's path. The beaches were littered with filth and rubbish.

Elizabeth shivered. It was so different here. They had an outside toilet or one could always use the byre if desperate, where the cows and calves were housed. The well was their own and they kept a trout in it to keep it clean. They seldom saw drunk people out their way.

The kettle was filled and hung on the hook for Robert and Arthur's return. She missed her son's frequent visits to the house for an oatcake during the morning or to fetch a tool to help someone in a job. She longed to know how he had got on.

In the late afternoon the door opened and in came Arthur.

"Well, lad," said his father, "sit down and tell us all your news."

"We had the Loard's Prayer first and we all had to repeat it. Then Mr Turnbull sang a hymn. He told us we had to speak very properly, like you said father. I wid redder spaek Shetlan."

"Na, you canna," said his sister who had been listening.

"Did you have enough to eat?" his mother asked.

"Yes, thanks," was the reply, "but we have to take a peat tomorrow to keep the fire going and money for paper and a pencil."

Arthur enjoyed school and being of a studious nature took in all he was taught. Mr Turnbull was very pleased with his pupils, especially Arthur who showed such an eagerness to learn. Each day as the child left home and wended his way to Lerwick, his mind was active. Several times he saw bodies on stretchers being taken for burial to the graveyard above the church. He decided he would become a doctor so that he could relieve the awful suffering and diseases the people died of.

Then again, he would witness fights and someone would be left on the ground in agony while the bully ran free. He would become a sheriff and sit at the bench in the Cockstoool giving out sentences to the offending persons.

When he entered the classroom and the Master started to speak and instruct him and his colleagues, he knew the best vocation for him was a teacher. With that 'lair' he could teach others to become wise and take up helpful professions.

"Yes," he thought as he walked up Baker's Closs to the classroom, "I'll just tell Mr Turnbull that I'll go in for a teacher so that I can help others like he does."

Arthur had just turned twelve when one day Mr Turnbull made an announcement to the class.

"As you know, I set up this private school to teach while I was waiting for an appointment as minister to a parish. That appointment has now come through. I have accepted it. I shall be very sorry to leave you all as you have proved to be attentive and industrious pupils. But as my calling is to the ministry, I felt bound to accept the offer. I trust you will all find vacancies elsewhere as education is a thing of the future. With it you can go far."

"I have written a letter to each of your parents regarding the situation and trust they will accept my apologies for not continuing to teach you. Feel free to visit me anytime. I shall continue to take an interest your careers and trust you will find the vocations to which you are suited."

The pupils shook hands with the Master and left but Arthur hung back. He could not believe this had really happened. Just as he was mapping out a career for himself the very person who could help him was vacating his post. How on earth was he to learn more? A tear escaped his eye which he hastily brushed away.

"Arthur, is something wrong? Have I upset you?" he was asked.

"No sir," began the tearful child. "I mean, yes. I had hopes of becoming a teacher like you but now I'll never be able to help other people if I can't learn." With that he broke down.

"Now, you must not make yourself ill over this. I am sure your father will be able to fit you in with another school."

"No sir. It's been a bad year for all with the loss of crops and I will not be able to go to another school. Father said I could stay as long as you were here."

"I see," said the now upset teacher. "I will call along your home on my way to Tingwall and leave some books for you to study. Many a student has come out brilliantly who has had to study himself. I shall keep in touch with you as you are my brightest pupil and I want to see you progressing. Now, off home."

Arthur walked home a very solemn boy. His wonderful world had collapsed around him. Oh well, he wasn't going to sit about and mope, he would devour the books Rev Turnbull brought to him and go on to teach himself to read, write and become efficient in maths.

"Why lad, what's the matter?" asked his father as he saw his son's disconsolate expression.

"Mr Turnbull has got his post in Tingwall so I can't go to school any more," was the answer. "But he says he'll give me books and help me as I can't go to another school. I'll have to earn money now."

"I'm afraid so," said Robert, sorry for the boy.

That night Robert and Elizabeth talked over the situation.

"I really can't afford to put Arthur to another school. There is such poverty this year. Meal is being brought into the islands and our potato crop has failed. He will have to get a job."

"And him so eager to learn," said Elizabeth.

Next morning Arthur ran to the well for water then got Bess ready to go to the peathill. She seemed to sense there was something wrong with her friend and kept very close to him as they walked up the hill. When Arthur sat down after filling the panniers he burst out crying, a thing he could not do at home in case anyone heard him. He felt a soft, warm, velvety nose on his neck and he turned and clung onto Bess. "At least someone knows how I feel," he told her. When they arrived back at the house Arthur put the peats beside the growing stack at the side of the house. He gave Bess a hug and an extra special brush down.

After breakfast he went to the beach to help the boys wash and lay out the fish. They asked why he was not at school that day so he told them what had happened.

"What way will you learn?" they asked him.

"Just try and help myself," was the answer.

One afternoon, Rev Turnbull called along Da Böd on his way to the country. Arthur saw him and washed his hands and came over to speak.

"These are some of the more advanced books we have not had a change to read yet, also some on arithmetic which you will find interesting I am sure. Now if you need any help at all please come out any time and see me. I shall welcome a visit."

As the minister left he thought what a pity that such a promising youth could not afford to be taught but he would certainly keep in touch and help all he could.

Arthur showed the books he had received to his parents who were delighted to think their son was capable of reading and learning for himself. That night he took his books and candle to the bedroom. As he left the room his mother said to him, "Don't read too long, it's bad for your eyes."

Interested to find out what the books contained, the boy chose one and sat at the little table in his room. He was very tired but had to discover what books he had been given.

Robert, on retiring, always checked the candles in the house to make sure that they had been snuffed out. Climbing the stairs to his son's room he found the candle had nearly burnt out and Arthur with his head on his hands sound asleep at the table! Robert lifted the sleeping boy and put him into his bed then eased off his boots and laid the 'wadmel' blanket over him, 'slocking' the light as he went out.

"Poor bairn," he said to his wife as he told her what he had done. "He's that anxious to learn."

Chapter 3

Work at Bressay

One morning, not long after Arthur had started working for his father again, Thomas Bolt called along Da Böd to speak to Robert Anderson. He had a fish-curing business on the island of Bressay. He noticed how Anderson's son worked tirelessly and methodically on the beach at Gremista and asked if he could employ the boy to help him in Bressay as he was a lad short.

"Certainly," answered Anderson, very pleased. "I am glad you asked because I feel it is better for a boy to be apprenticed elsewhere rather than by his own family."

"I was watching him at work," said Thomas Bolt, "and he does very well. When can he come to me?"

"Anytime. His tutor, Rev Turnbull, has had word that the post at Tingwall is now vacant so Arthur has had to leave school. I shall call him to come and speak to you."

"Arthur!" called his father. "Clean your hands and come and speak to Mr Bolt. He would like you to work for him in Bressay – just the same as you are doing here."

Mr Bolt informed Arthur that he would need to stay in the huts provided for the other beach boys as they started work early in the mornings. That evening Robert rowed his son across to Heogan on Bressay where the huts were situated. Elizabeth was very upset to see her son leave but times were hard and something extra was always welcome.

For Arthur it was very different from home life. It was cold and dark in the early mornings as the sun rose behind the island, casting long shadows on the beach. Looking towards Lerwick the houses were bathed in sunshine. Arthur missed the walks up the peathill before breakfast with dear Bess or carrying in the water for his mother. However, his sister was seeing to a lot of the work helping her mother.

Boats arriving with fish would land their catch on the beach at Heogan then the men would split the ling leaving them for the boys to scrub clean in the sea before carrying them to the salting vats. When the fish had been thoroughly salted they were carried to the beach and spread out on the shingle to dry in the sun. On warm days the fish dried quickly but if it rained they all had to be collected together into bundles and covered over with huge tarpaulins. It was heavy work and cold and the boys' hands would be cracked and sore working with the salt. The fish was exported to Spain.

When all the fish had been covered over on wet days the beach boys gathered in their huts but Arthur would go into the office and read one of his books or watch the man at work at the desk writing down the skipper's name of each boat as it discharged and adding the number of fish landed beside it. He was fascinated by the figures and quickly learnt how to add and calculate the costs.

Arthur was an amenable boy and got on well with everyone .

Mr Bolt took notice of the boy's interest in the financial side of affairs and eventually asked him to work in the office. This was a great step forward. Working in close proximity each day brought a friendship between the employer and his assistant.

"Arthur, I suppose you have noticed that James Hay supplies us with a lot of dried fish which we export. He also gets timber from Norway which is so much needed in the islands for buildings, fencing posts and, especially, for boats. James and his sons have the new shop at the south side of the Tolbooth. It is not far from the house he built in Church Lane – Bonavista. He had a weaving factory at Catfirth and at Bleachfield but they were not successful. Pity. Shetlanders can be stubborn folks and like things as they always have been so do not think he got much help from them in the factory.

"I must order some timber for Fetlar. Next time you are in Lerwick will you go along Magnus Hughson's in Park Lane and give him this note to tell him to collect goods from my store for the North Isles Trader to deliver next time she sails.

"I see James Mouat of Hamarsland has finished his house at Da Cockstool on the lower side of the street, at the sooth end. He has a cellar and lodberry with it too. He built the houses in South Kirk Closs. With each house goes the right to have a pew in the parish kirk. So, that will do for today."

In the store beside the office at Cruister were all types of food and hardware. Many and varied were the articles ordered and despatched. Arthur Nicolson had a store in Lerwick which supplied Heogan which, in turn, supplied a large 'flit boat' going to the island of Fetlar. Arthur became quite adept at calculating the figures and Mr Bolt soon promoted him to the job of clerk.

Each day Arthur went to the store to check on goods which had been delivered the previous day. He also made a note of stock to be ordered. The store always smelt of tar from the barrels just inside the door and timber from Norway for making boats. Huge three-legged pots stood on the floor.

These were used for heating tar to cover felt on the roofs or for keeping fires burning in the large six-oared boats going to the 'haaf' fishing. They went out to sea till only the tops of the hills could be seen.

Hooks and lines were on shelves with 'owskerries' for bailing out the boats. Coarse material for sails were in bundles alongside pots of 'cootch' or bark for preserving the sails and which gave them their tan colour. There were hammers, boxes of nails, shovels and picks for work on the roads also barrows for the croftwork.

Sacks of beremeal stood alongside salt, some of which was used for preserving mutton and fish. Among the goods ordered were course socks for the fishermen and Dutchmen to wear in their clogs. Household items included biscuits, sugar, tea, bottles of aniseed, soap, combs made of bone and horn, kettles, pots, tobacco and gin. Cloth, striped and plan also red flannel for the womens' petticoats. Needles of bone and knitting 'wires' or needles for the women to knit socks as they sat at home or travelled the hillside.

One morning Arthur asked Mr Bolt why the herring were so plentiful in and around Shetland.

"Well," began Thomas Bolt, "the herring lay their eggs at the bottom of the sea and it has to be deep enough so that the spawning grounds are safe from any disturbance on the surface or currents, so that the immature fish can thrive undisturbed. The warm sea from the Gulf Stream surrounds Britain and on the east cost it is sheltered from the Atlantic breakers. It's about a hundred fathoms deep. The herring grounds stretch from Yarmouth to Shetland. The herring is a wonderful fish as it can live at the bottom of the sea under tremendous pressure or come to the surface. It is long shaped so it can swim fast. It's really a beautiful thing, all colours just like a starling's breast."

"I never thought of it like that," said the boy smiling.

Many boats entered and left the harbour each day. Boats of foreign nationality, some calling for water, others for fish or fresh supplies. Warships often visited as they checked the waters around the outlying islands. Britain was still at war with Napoleon.

The dread of any Shetlander was when a navy ship appeared and lowered a small boat containing sailors who would row ashore and go to each house demanding that men and young boys join their crew. The Press Gang took many a young unsuspecting boy going about his duty.

One morning as usual Arthur entered the office and started to write up his ledgers. A shadow darkened the doorway and in a second a sailor had descended on the lad holding him in a vice-like grip. Next he was marched from the office down to the beach and put on a boat to be taken to the ship.

By this time some of the boys had disappeared to the far side of the islands hiding anywhere they could. Some in barns, others in lofts. The sailors were relentless in their search – even entering the cottages and taking men from their beds.

Mr Bolt arrived at the office and finding no trace of Arthur and hearing shouts from the receding boat realised that his clerk was onboard. He shouted to the sailors to stop rowing and bring their captive back at once or he would send the law after them. The boy was under-age and they would have to pay for their misdeeds if he was not returned at once.

The boat was duly turned and Arthur released. Mr Bolt explained to the officer that the boy was very fond of the sea and intended joining the navy next year. As he, Mr Bolt, was employed by Lord Dundas and Arthur was his clerk, he thought it would not look good if word got to Lord Dundas that one of his employees had been taken by the press gang.

Arthur would no doubt have been anxious to see on board the naval vessel but what would his dear parents have done if he had been taken from them in such a crude manner? What would kind Mr Bolt have done without him in the office? He determined to settle down again and work as hard as ever until next year when he was able to volunteer, willingly, for a job in the navy.

He heard tales of a nasty incident in one of the country districts when the press gang entered the house of a Mrs Urscilla Smith. Lieutenant Wilson led the gang into the house where she lived with her mother and three brothers. It was early morning. Wilson's men held lit candles which the women blew out. A battle ensued in which the family were severely injured. Dr Edmonston dressed their wounds.

Mr Bolt often had business to attend to in Lerwick so Arthur would row his employer over to the town. It was quite a distance for a young boy but he enjoyed it wending his way through the different vessels anchored in the sound. On hot days his feet would stick to the tar on the tilfers or floor boards and his head would be baked in the sun.

One day he was heard to say that he wished the sound was not so broad! The little rowing boat would leave Heogan and cross the sound to the steps below Lochend House – it was over a mile. While Thomas Bolt was seeing to business, Arthur would go to Gremista to see his folks and catch up with all their news. He missed most of all the happy times in the evenings when the day's work was done and he and his family would sit round the peat fire. He loved to watch his mother as she sat knitting, spinning or baking on the open hearth. She was an expert knitter and made lace shawls, scarves and stockings. The heavier wool was used to knit socks, jumpers, mittens and gloves. When she went to the peathill or to fetch the cow for milking, she always took her knitting or 'sock' as it is called to this day. Her daughter also had learned to knit from an early age and when they sold their goods it brought in a welcome income.

While the women knitted father brought down his fiddle from the hook on the wall to play Shetland reels or dances. Neighbours loved to visit and many an old story was told of experiences in the whaling days or out at the fishing in small boats and heavy seas. It was usually well past midnight when the party broke up. Arthur would not sit idle either. He would carve a piece of wood for a tooth for the rake or mend the wooden handle of a croft implement and in doing so became a skilful woodworker. He also loved music and sometimes accompanied his father on the fiddle. Now his great love was reading.

Arriving early at the house some days his father would say, "What about a visit to Tingwall to see Rev Turnbull today? It won't take us long to walk out there and back before you have to row Mr Bolt back to Bressay." "Yes, father," the boy would reply, "I would like that. There are several things that puzzle me and only my tutor can help me. I do enjoy reading and tackling the maths problems but it is better to have expert advice."

Elizabeth always gave them a bag of food to sustained them on their journey. They would put it in a large bag and sling it over the shoulder on a stick. Taking their collie dog, they followed the path up the hill and past the peatbanks then down into the valley of Dale, rising up the other side to the Windy Grind. On a fine day they could see the distant isles in the sunshine – Whalsay and the Skerries. Looking eastwards, they noted the point of Kebister Ness where they often walked, the hill of Tagdale, the burn of Frakkafield and the cottages near the burn of Dale. They passed two cottages at Dale on the west side as they made their way over the crown of the next hill. This took them past the north end of the Loch of Tingwall and to the church and manse where Rev Turnbull stayed.

Nearing their destination, Robert explained why the district was named Tingwall. The 'ting' in the old Norse days was the name given to the parliament which was held on the small peninsula at the north end of the loch. This was in the days before Earl Patrick Stewart built his castle in Scalloway where he held court. When two people had a dispute, the offending person was allowed to go free if he could run as far as the church from the peninsula but the snag was that the persons in the then ruling council impeded his progress by hitting him with sticks and kicking him and he was fortunate to make it to the church.

Rev Turnbull was delighted to see his visitors and ordered a meal to be set before them before they started work. He was amazed at the progress young Anderson had made on his own and was able to instruct him further in his studies. Many subjects, both educational and local, were discussed by the time the pair took their leave to walk the three miles home.

Winters are hard in the northern isles and in Shetland many animals died in the hills unable to find food owing to the thick snow drifts. Ponies and sheep were found dead in the springtime and this was a great loss to the crofters as they depended on the meat of the sheep or the wool for the women to knit. The little Shetland ponies, though small, are very sturdy and can carry great weights. As this was the only form of transport on the ground they were in much demand especially for visitors from outwith the islands who preferred to ride rather than walk. Sometimes the Dutchmen used the little 'Shelties' for riding in a park as exercise after being cooped up in their boats for long periods.

When Arthur was at home he often took supplies out to the visiting boats in the harbour. Many a neighbour he helped with their spring or harvest work along with that of his own parents. He could not bear to see anyone in trouble. With a nature like his, he was never idle for long.

"Mother and I will come with you to Lerwick today, Arthur, as she has some knitted goods to sell," said Robert one morning. Arriving in town, the family walked to the south end of the street, as far as Bain's Court to see Murdoch Brown who was a butcher and shoemaker and sold calf skins for leather.

"My wife would like a leather knitting belt," said Robert as he chose one of the leathers on the counter.

"Which colour would you prefer ma'am?" asked Murdoch.

"I think brown please," answered Elizabeth, "it will be different to the old one I made many years ago from gull quills bound together."

"I'll take this piece of leather," said Robert. "We have plenty of Bess's hair to stuff it with. Could you punch holes in it Murdoch please for the needles and I'll need some thonging to sew it up? Thanks."

After they left the shop Robert remembered he had to buy a new tushkar with which to cut the peats. Arthur was old enough to learn and it was best to have one of his own.

"We'll go to Andrew Peterson and buy a tushkar and also a corn hook. That will come in handy at harvest time. Let's go in and see Jock Murray before we leave the court as I want him to make a couple of wooden boxes for our meal. He is a good joiner. Like myself, he was once captured by the press gang but managed to escape by telling the men he was a Custom's

House Officer and was on his way to make an arrest! He said he was a King's man himself. He worked for James Bain, the auctioneer!"

No doubt Arthur enjoyed telling his parents of his escapade with the press gang and how Mr Bolt was able to free him again. A whole year seemed an eternity away as he thought of sailing in one of those large boats in the Royal Navy.

By the time Arthur was ready to leave work, Mr Bolt had trained up another boy to take his place. His employer was sad at the thought of losing his expert clerk, especially as they had become friends as well as employer and employee. It was a sad parting but as the boy was leaving, Bolt put his hand on the boy's shoulder and gave him some advice, "Dö weel and persevere."

Arthur took this advice to heart.

Chapter 4

To Sea at Last

Now that Arthur had come of age to join the navy he knew his time had come to leave Shetland. For months now he had been saving up his money in case a boat came into the harbour and he could get a berth in her to take him south. He had his wooden kist with his clothes and books all ready to go.

"When we go to town tomorrow," Robert told his son, "we shall call along Robert Davidson, the watchmaker, and you can choose a time-piece for yourself."

"But father, I can tell the time by the sun and the stars," replied the boy.

"Yes lad, you can here, but when you leave the islands and go south the sun will have different positions. Robert will have a fine watch and your mother and I would like you to have it as a keepsake when you are away."

"That is very kind of you father," said the youngster," but I can assure you I will never need anything to remind me of my loved ones and home."

Having a message for Thomas Bolt next day, Robert and his son left Gremista and made their way into town. As they neared the south end, they stopped at Davidson's shop and went in to purchase Arthur's watch. He was very proud of it and it would serve him well in the years to come.

"Your mother and I will miss you greatly," said his father, "but always remember the good advice given to you by Thomas Bolt."

"You will also need a jacket and trousers for going onboard the ship so we will look into Walter Irvine at Annsbrae Cottages. I think he will be best to fit you out."

When a visiting warship called his father suggested they row out to the boat and speak to the captain. Arthur was welcomed onboard. He was told the ship was sailing for Portsmouth where he would be informed which ship he was to join.

His mother was heartbroken to see her boy leaving the islands and wondered if ever she would see him again. When in Bressay, he sometimes called in to see them but this was different. Would he remember to write home? Did he have enough money till he earned a proper wage? Would he choose the right company to keep? Elizabeth vowed to pray each day for her son that he would be kept safe from all dangers.

Many women got into small boats and rowed out to the warship to plead with their sons or husbands to come home but it was to no avail, once onboard they were forbidden to go ashore. It was going to be a hard life for the lads who had known only the freedom of the country around them but life was hard and some would benefit from the discipline meted out to them. Elizabeth busied herself about the house to keep her mind off the retreating boat. She fed the hens and the geese, helped her daughter collect eggs then went up the peathill with Bess as an excuse to see the ship disappearing by the town. She sat down and wept. How she loved her bairns and now that was one of them away.

"Come Bess," she said drying her eyes, "I'll fill the panniers and we'll go home." The little pony seemed to sense the loss of her friend and kept very close to Elizabeth as they descended the hill to the house.

"I think we'll go to Vatsland," she said to her daughter when she got home," and see how Anne Gray is progressing with your frock. "Shall we?"

"Yae Midder," said the girl running for her shawl.

When they arrived at the cottage they were given tea and an oatcake then shown the finished frock and Barbara was delighted with it.

"Can I wear it tae da kirk on Sunday?" she asked.

"Yes," answered her mother very proud of the pretty dress.

Elizabeth paid for the frock – half in money and the rest in wool she had spun, also milk and butter, as Anne had no means of making these herself.

As the weeks went by the parents waited anxiously for news of their son. One day there was a letter, it was like gold – very precious. It told of Arthur's journey to Portsmouth and how he and the other new crew members had got on. He had been given a job on a sloop to begin with then on the *Ardent*, a vessel of ninety-four guns going to the Baltic. Being a good sailor, Arthur enjoyed the life but some of the lads were very ill and did not make good seamen at all. Life onboard was very exciting with not a dull moment.

Robert Anderson missed his son and kept up a correspondence with him all the time he was away. Many a time it was the news from home that kept the boy going. However, it was an expensive exercise being one shilling and sixpence for a letter, nine pence paid by the sender and nine pence by the receiver. Many a meal Arthur missed on account of sending or receiving a letter. Sometimes it took him all his time and wit to make a few pence for the postage.

When Arthur was promoted to midshipman in 1809 no-one was prouder of his achievement than his former teacher, Rev John Turnbull. Thomas Bolt felt the boy was missing out on his career just being a ship's clerk so he wrote to John Dick who influenced the boy's promotion to officer. He saw much active service in the war.

As a midshipman, and being in close contact with the officers onboard the ship, Arthur observed everything in a quiet way and soon took in all the details of how a ship was run. Still anxious to advance his education he learnt Spanish and Portuguese and became quite fluent in both languages. He never tired of reading and all this knowledge was to stand him in good stead in years to come.

Most of the officers onboard the *Ardent* were from well-to-do families and well used to spending money on luxuries and drink but Arthur was not of the same category. He had attained his status through dogged hard work. He found the going hard as regards financial affairs and had to succumb eventually to asking to be demoted. He was accordingly transferred to the *Bermuda* in 1810 as captain's clerk. She was a small ship of only ten guns but this suited him fine.

This situation did not last long as the war with France came to an end with the capture of Napoleon and his imprisonment on the island of Elba. Arthur and his mates were paid-off. He made his way to London to try and secure a job there, walking approximately eighty miles. Being a Shetlander, Arthur could turn his hand to most jobs and was a skilful carpenter. However, jobs were few and far between and many a day he went hungry existing on bread, cheese and port or water.

A letter from Robert cheered Arthur up. "You will be glad to hear that James Ross, the postmaster, has been appointed session clerk and presenter at the Lerwick Parish Church. Someone donated money for the education of poor boys in Lerwick and the Kirk Session has appointed James Ross to look after affairs.

"I was at Ollasons getting a pair of shoes mended and spoke to Willie Sinclair. He misses his brother who was drowned. He still lives at the little house on Sinclair's beach. It's a wonder the sea has not washed it away with the high tides. I also called along Andrew Smith at Candle House in Gardie Court. They make the best candles. He is a fine soul Andrew.

"I must call along Hance Jamieson and see if he will sweep our chimneys. The old 'lums' in the country were never swept unless with a heather besom.

"When mother was at Vatsland today she learned of the death of David Kay. He and Gideon Bruce were hauling in their handlines when their boat overturned. The boat was between the auld House of Kebister and the Holm of Vatsland. Gideon survived but David's body was picked up later. What a tragedy. He leaves a family of six.

"I hear that Peter Leslie from Dunrossness has left the sea and bought the North Ness. He is making in into a farm after a lot of hard work. He is doing up the old piers and yards so they will be ready for the summer when the fishing starts again.

"Your sister is hoping to marry John Morrison. His wife Cathie died. He built the Victoria warehouse and pier. He first came to Lerwick to re-build the Fort with Robert Deans who lives at Leog. Do you remember we often used to chat to them at the Fort on your way to school. Little did I think then that he would become my son-in-law! I hope he and Barbara will be very happy.

"The bellman today had some bad news. Apparently, Donald Robertson of Eshaness had asked Laurence Tulloch of Clothister for some epsom salts. Whether Laurence had mixed the tins we do not know but the powder he gave Donald was nitre. The poor man was dead within five hours.

"Do you remember the old well in Mounthooly Street? Well they now have a pump there so the folks do not have to 'demble' their buckets in now. It is much better and cleaner and Simon Laurenson who has the smithy near-by is being paid to look after it.

"George Laurenson of South Farm Clickimin was in trouble with the law lately. He refused to hire his gig to a party going to Tingwall. R. L. Stevenson was one of them. I must say I always find him very helpful when I hire him. Old Mansie Mode has retired from being the Sheriff Officer and I believe that George Leask is getting the job. He and his wife, Rose, live in that little thatched cottage at the South End. He has to ring the Tolbooth bell at 9.00pm so that the shopkeepers know that they have to close their shops. I bought a couple of lamps today, also paraffin, for lighting. They are so much brighter than candles.

"Peter Sievwright, who lives at the foot of Navy Lane, has started a bake shop, the first in Lerwick. The town's folk call the lane 'Baker's Close'. He certainly knows how to make money. He lets some of his rooms to the soldiers from Fort Charlotte. I hear some complaints that he charges too much for the meal and potatoes. He bakes good bread and biscuits, not that we buy them often as mother is a good cook.

"I hear of the death of Gideon Gifford of Busta. He married Grizel Nicolson of Lochend."

One letter which really excited Arthur was written in 1811. It contained the news that Rev Turnbull had married the daughter of his deceased predecessor. She was Wilhelmina Sands. They lived in the manse at Tingwall where Arthur and his father had visited his former teacher.

In 1812, Arthur received a letter telling of famine again in the islands. He remembered the last time in 1804 when he had had to leave school because times were so hard he could not continue his education which meant so much to him but had to work as a beach boy at Heogan. What a lot had transpired since then. He felt deeply sorry for any youngsters who were in the same position. He was grateful to Rev Turnbull for his help at school also the times when he and his father set off on foot for Tingwall to see his tutor and gain more information for his education.

When news of Napoleon's escape from Elba reached London, Arthur knew that war would soon break out again so he collected what possessions he had. Tying them in a large handkerchief, he slung it over his shoulder on a pole and trudged the eighty miles back to Portsmouth. He was footsore and weary when he arrived. One of his former shipmates, hardly recognising him, helped him to the shipping office to sign on for a place on a ship. He said, "You look all-in, what have you bee doing with yourself?"

So poor Arthur told his friend the story of his time in the city. Thanks to his friend, he got a job on the *Bermuda* again with regular meals and with pay was able to write home more often.

Letters collected from the Post Office in London were handed to the crew after the ship had left for the Baltic. It was always a joy for Arthur to receive a letter from Shetland especially one from his father. As Arthur looked at the envelope handed to him his face clouded in concern. The envelope was black-edged denoting the death of a relative or close friend. The boy took the letter to his sleeping quarters so that he might have peace to read it. His eyes filled with tears as he read the familiar hand-writing.

"Dear Arthur,

"It is incumbent upon me to write and tell you sad news. Your dear Mother has been taken from us. I cannot believe it even now. A week past she felt unwell with a severe pain in her side. It seems the doctor could do nothing to help her. Yesterday she passed away in her sleep.

"I know you will grieve son as you were so close to each other. I shall miss her very much. She was a caring, loving and dutiful wife and mother.

"However, your sister Barbara is coping very well with the household chores and the animals. It is a great pity you are so far away at this time. As always John Turnbull has been a tower of strength to us helping in any way that he can.

"God bless you and keep you safe,

"Affectionately yours,

"Father."

Many friends came to comfort Robert in his grief. He sometimes sat and thought of those first days when he and Elizabeth came to Da Böd. They had been so happy with the new spacious house and their little family. They had entertained many friends, also important people connected with the fishing industry.

One of Elizabeth's friends who was deeply touched with her death was Catherine Johnson. Catherine often helped Barbara giving her advice about household affairs. It was during one of these visits about two years later that Robert realised what a genuinely kind person Catherine was, having helped them in their bereavement. More than that she had continued to care and help in an unobtrusive way.

Robert realised one day that he was falling deeply in love with this unselfish, devoted woman. One evening as Catherine put her shawl round her shoulders to pay a visit to Anne Gray at Vatsland, Robert said on impulse, "Would you like it if I accompanied you?"

Catherine, blushing, answered, "That would be very nice as it is quite a long way to go on my own. It will be fine to have company."

Arriving at the cottage Catherine settled up with Anne for some sewing she had done for her. When the couple left the cottage Robert suggested a walk to Kebister ness and Dales Voe to see the sunset on the west-side, as it was such a beautiful evening.

Sitting on the heather-clad hillside Robert turned to Catherine and said, "I have been amazed and touched by the competent way you have helped Barbara in the house since Elizabeth was taken from us. Thinking things over I feel I could not cope without your help and kindly advice."

Catherine smiled, "That is so kind of you Robert. I loved Elizabeth and felt I had to encourage Barbara as she seemed so young to take on the responsibility of running the large house."

Robert took Catherine's hand in his. "Catherine," he began hesitantly, "I have come to love you and trust you and would be so happy if you felt the same for me."

Catherine put her other hand over Robert's and leaning her head on his shoulder she whispered, "And I love you with all my heart too."

The couple smiled then sealed their love with a kiss.

As Anne Gray shut the hen-house door for the night she smiled as she saw the silhouette of the couple arm in arm disappear over the hilltop on their way to Gremista.

The next letter Arthur received from his father told him of his acquaintance with Catherine Johnson and how they hoped to be married in the spring time.

By 1815, Arthur felt he had had enough of life at sea and quit the navy. Surprisingly, he made for London again. However, things turned out differently for him this time.

Chapter 5

Success

In London, Arthur was fortunate to get a job as a copying clerk. Another letter arrived and this time Arthur read and re-read it. Apparently, his mother's brother, Peter Ridland, had recently settled in London. He mentioned that he would be pleased to see his nephew any time. It did not take Arthur long to find his uncle's address where he was warmly welcomed. On one visit, his uncle introduced him to Christopher Hill, a shipowner, who, hearing that Arthur could speak Spanish and Portuguese fluently, introduced him to another friend, Brodie Willcox, a ship broker.

The latter asked Arthur to come as clerk to him in his office as he seemed to have a good grasp of the Spanish language and the customs of the countries he was dealing with.

Arthur Anderson proved to be a great help to Willcox in his business. So much so that he was taken into the firm as a partner in 1822.

Although Arthur Anderson was very busy with helping in the floating of the new company he still kept his mind alert to the poverty in Shetland. He felt it would be wonderful for the people of the islands to find out what was going on in the rest of the country. Maybe he could send some helpful hints on farming, etc. by starting a monthly newspaper. When it came out it was called *The Shetland Journal*. It contained Liberal political views and was mostly written by Anderson himself.

The same year he founded another company on the island of Vaila on the west coast, called The Shetland Fishing Company.

The lairds in Shetland 'ruled the roost' completely and Arthur found it very unpleasant as he thought of his fellow fishermen always in debt. How well he knew the situation himself. Nothing to reward the men for the hours spent fishing on the cold, dark nights and stormy waters, the lairds going off with most of the catch and the fishermen's families starving.

Arthur had seen fish dried on wooden pallets and they seemed superior to those dried on the shingle or stones as done in Shetland. He tried this procedure in Vaila but as they say, 'tradition dies hard' and in this case, Shetland won, going back to the old system. The venture only lasted a few years before being wound-up.

Robert had told his son a couple of years before that the 'Old Kirk' in

Lerwick was deemed unsafe and a new one was being built at the foot of the road to the Knab. Writing in 1829 he said that the 'New Kirk' had now been opened and it weas impressive.

A year later, his son received this letter. "You will be interested to hear that Thomas Bolt, your old employer, has sold his house at Cruister to William Mouat of Gardie and is now residing in Commercial Street in a house above Sinclair's beach. Bolt hired James Smith, the boatman, to help ferry his goods to Lerwick from Bressay. The flitboats with six to eight oars can carry a lot more than the small four-oared boats.

"Did you hear that Clunie Ross, who lived at Weisdale, is developing the Cocos Islands into a coconut plantation? He calls himself 'King of the Cocos Islands'. He always did think a lot of himself.

"The town of Lerwick has been created at Burgh so magistrates can now be appointed. I hear policemen will be coming soon and much need to keep law and order. Young children roaming the streets and lanes are doing a lot of damage.

"Councillors have been appointed. They have employed scavengers to clean up the streets and lanes, which were in a disgraceful mess. They have been provided with barrows, spades and brooms to help them in their work.

"Commercial Street is to be paved with stone slabs three and a half inches thick. It will be much better than the sodden earth. You'll never know the old town!"

When Christopher Hill first met Arthur he liked the forthright way of the young man and his eagerness to get ahead.

Hill invited him to his house to meet his wife and family of three daughters. Arthur often visited the house and, in time, fell in love with the eldest daughter, Mary Ann. Seeing he was now partner in the firm of Willcox and Anderson, he felt confident to ask Mary Ann to marry him knowing he had the means to support a wife in the manner to which she was accustomed. They were married in 1822 and made their home at 'The Grove', Norwood, Surrey.

As usual, Arthur's thoughts were soaring ahead of his everyday duties. In 1825, he heard of a small American schooner that had gone aground near Dover. He suggested to Willcox that they buy her, fit her out with guns and use her for trading to Portugal. "Our own ship! Why not?" he asked.

The proposition was carefully thought over and duly carried out. Arthur sailed with the schooner on her first voyage to Portugal. On his return he discussed the trip with his partner.

"Willcox, have you heard the latest?"

"No Anderson, I have not but I know you are dying to tell me."

"Well," answered the excited Anderson, "you know that Brunel has been working on steam for years now? Do you not think that steam would help our voyages to the Peninsula and beyond to be faster and a lot safer?"

"Yes, I have thought about steam travel. I agree with the faster side of it but am a bit dubious about the safer side of the project."

"Should we have a ship built for sail and steam then?"

"Yes," answered a tolerant Willcox, "all in good time."

Arthur left his partner's office sure in the knowledge that his next suggestion to help the mails have a quicker delivery would be accepted. He smiled as he walked to his private office remembering his father saying those exact works to him as he had expressed the desire to sail in one of the tall ships in the Lerwick Harbour. He must have been about seven years old then.

Willcox shook his head as his partner shut the door behind him.

"Whatever will the man think of next?" he asked himself, "it's a jolly good idea though and I must admit it had crossed my mind several times but with things going as they are I would not like to disrupt the service in any way."

Meanwhile, at Arthur's office, things were going ahead at a great rate. First of all, they would need to get in touch with the Royal Mail and see if they approved of the bags going by steam ship. A ship would need to be chartered as there was not time to build one. Delays and more delays!! He spoke to their ally, Richard Bourne, whose family ran a steamship line from Dublin. Richard was able to charter the *William Fawcett* for them in 1835. Unfortunately, the Admiralty would not give consent at this time for the mails to be carried.

While in Portugal on business Arthur Anderson heard of the death of the Portugese sovereign, King John VI. He was succeeded by Pedro IV who gave up the crown in favour of his infant daughter Dóna Maria. He stipulated that she would become queen if she married her uncle Dom Miguel of Spain who was appointed regent in the meantime. However Dom Miguel contrived to get himself declared king in 1828 by the Cortes, the ruling parliament of Portugal and Spain.

Civil war broke out and anarchy followed until 1832 when Dom Pedro now governor of Brazil and father of Dóna Maria, landed at Oporto. Civil war broke out in Portugal about 1825 when reactionaries tried to dethrone the Queen. Admiral Sir Charles Napier, or 'Mad Charlie', as he was commonly known in the navy, offered to form a navy for her. When Arthur heard of the injustice to the crown he started gun-running for the Queen. As this was an illicit operation, he took the name of Mr Smith. The firm chartered a small ship for the job and Arthur managed to smuggle out two of the Queen's leaders to England. They raised money for the Queen's cause and, it being successful, the Queen was returned to the throne.

In 1832, civil war broke out in Spain and, being a true Shetlander, what could Arthur do but take his chartered ship and enter into the fray again.

As a result of the help given to the Queen of Portugal by the firm of Willcox and Anderson, they were rewarded for their services by various favours in the trade between the two countries.

The company was also rewarded for their services by being allowed to use the colours of Spain and Portugal on their flag. The royal red and yellow of Spain and the blue and white of Portugal.

The *William Fawcett* was the first ship to fly the flag. Voyages by steamship were duly advertised to the Peninsula. A great movement of faith on the part of the partners of Willcox and Anderson.

In a few years time, the company had several ships. They also secured the government mail contract to the Peninsula.

The 22nd August, 1837 was marked as the official date for the flotation of the Peninsula Steam Navigation Company.

Chapter 6

The *Don Juan*

Having secured the Government contract to carry the mails to Spain and Portugal, Willcox and Anderson ordered their flagship *Don Juan*, the largest of the fleet, to sail to Gibraltar.

"What about sailing with me this time?" asked Arthur of his wife. "You would enjoy the voyage and it would be a wonderful time to relax away from your many duties at home?"

"Yes," answered Mary Ann, "I would like that. But what shall I wear?"

"Something warm and not too voluminous. It will be breezy on deck so take a hat you can tie on so it does not blow off!"

"I shall go and look out some suitable clothes then," said Mary Ann leaving the room. It was going to be a great experience for her to travel abroad. Sometimes she envied her husband the long voyages to the Continent and longed to go with him. Now was her chance.

Besides clothes and shoes, Mary Ann chose a few books and her sewing and embroidery. There would be no idle days like the sailing ships when they were becalmed because of lack of wind. Steam was the future way of propelling ships along and they usually made landings in record time.

On 1st September, 1837, the *Don Juan* was scheduled to sail on their first government contract voyage.

"Are you ready?" shouted Arthur upstairs to his wife. "The carriage is at the door to take us to the pier."

"Do I look alright in this outfit?" a nervous wife asked.

"You look wonderful," said Arthur admiring Mary Ann's choice of coat and hat as she sailed down the stairs. Long gloves covered her hands and she carried a larger leather bag containing personal possessions such as rings, necklaces, brooches, glasses and a little money.

Arriving at the dock, they emerged from the carriage and approached the gangway. Once onboard a steward led them to a luxurious cabin.

"I see you remembered my request," Arthur said to the young man. I asked for a P.O.S.H. cabin and we have got one""

"A what?" asked his mystified wife.

"A P.O.S.H. cabin," repeated her husband. "If our cabin is on the port side going out then we will be able to see land all the time and our cabin be in the shade from the sun and, on returning, we will be on the starboard side coming home. So, it's Port Out and Starboard Home – in short, P.O.S.H . Not bad?"

"You and Brodie are great for your abbreviations," laughed Mary Ann.

The journey to Gibraltar was uneventful. The meals onboard were delicious with a varied menu. The dining saloon was beautiful as were the other saloons. Quite luxurious.

Arriving at Gibraltar, the mails were the first to be landed. Arthur heaved a sigh of relief to see them safely on dry land but he felt anxious about them reaching their destinations in time and intact. He felt a gentle nudge on his arm and a voice said, "Are we alighting here?"

"Sorry, my dear," he said turning to his wife, "I was just wondering when these mails will reach their destinations."

"You have done your part of the deal, now come on – I'm longing to see Gibraltar."

"You are quite right there," said Arthur taking his wife's arm as they descended to the cabin to collect their bags, but a new notion had struck Arthur which he was sure would be of great advantage to getting the mails to their desired ports in one voyage.

Two weeks later the mails for Britain were put onboard and the *Don Juan* duly sailed for her home port.

Not long after leaving port Arthur went up on deck to speak to Captain Engledue.

"We came out in record time," he observed, "do you think we shall be able to repeat that on the homeward journey?"

"Might do," said the Captain, "but I see a lot of fog about."

Arthur went below again to wait for the dinner gong. He told his wife, "John says we should make good headway on the return voyage. It is very foggy out now but if Engledue keeps to the rules we should be all right. I shall write home and tell father of this wonderful achievement. He will be so proud of ..."

Arthur never finished his sentence. He heard a voice shouting to him to come on deck.

"We've hit the rocks," someone shouted.

The fog had descended and it surrounded the ship like a huge blanket.

"We've struck the rocks," said Engledue in desperation, "we'll get anchors off so that we can secure the ship to the rocks and make sure she does not slip into deeper water."

"There's a passing Spanish ship. Hail her and we'll get the mail off onto her," shouted Anderson. Speaking fluent Spanish he was able to persuade the ship to come alongside and lift the mails safely onboard. He rushed to the cabin and told Mary Ann to grab her bag and come at once, they were going on the Spanish ship to deliver the mails safely on shore and try to talk someone into helping the stricken vessel.

Mary Ann picked up her bag and started to look for clothes.

"Come, hurry," said Arthur agitatedly, "you have no time to take anything else. We must think of the other passengers on board."

Mary Ann just had time to snatch her pretty pale blue velvet coat and bonnet with the white fur before following her husband up the now leaning stairway. She managed, with some difficulty, to descend the ladder and jump into the waiting boat.

The *Don Juan* was listing now and Arthur feared they might not be back in time to rescue the rest of the passengers. It was a mystery to him how Engledue had misjudged his bearings. He was the best captain in the fleet of ships and this was the finest ship afloat.

On arriving at the pier at Tarifa, about 20 miles from Gibraltar, the mails were transferred to HMS *Asia*, sailing shortly for England. Arthur, Mary Ann, two passengers and the Admiralty messenger stepped ashore and went immediately to the shipping office. They were not very co-operative at first, it was a blessing that Arthur could speak and argue with them in Spanish. However, after a long period, they gave their consent for a boat to go and collect the stranded passengers. Everyone was taken off the listing ship and brought to land. Captain Engledue arranged for the stewards to find accommodation for the passengers until another ship was available to take them back to England.

Captain Engledue did all he possibly could to help, fearing all the time that this was to be the last time he would captain a ship. He was very upset but Arthur assured him that he would do all he could to persuade the authorities that what had happened was an unavoidable accident. He won the case.

Chapter 7

Knitwear Boost

A s Arthur sat one evening watching his wife embroidering, he thought back to the times when his mother and sister sat at the big open fire at Da Böd knitting and spinning the Shetland wool. It was quite a process. Wool from the sheep, which had been rooed in the summer, was kept in sacks in the barn. A quantity was taken out and kept in the house near the fire. One of them would tease out the 'oo', as the raw wool is called, and comb it between two cairds to make it smooth and remove any tufts of grass or heather. It was rolled into a 'rolag' – a long shape, ready for the other person to spin. When knitting they each wore a leather belt stuffed with horse hair, about eight inches long, and three inches wide, in which one of their needles were pushed to keep the knitting even and the tension correct.

They knitted scarves, socks, berets, gloves and shawls and sold them to the shops or bartered them for food. An idea struck Arthur (nothing new for him), as he thought of all the beautiful garments produced in the islands. The garments could be sent to Edinburgh, London or, better still, why not present some samples to Her Majesty Queen Victoria! As he pondered this new venture, he felt it could easily come off and once royalty accepted Shetland knitting, others were bound to follow suit.

That evening, he wrote home asking if enquiries could be made into purchasing garments for the project. If it took off then it would greatly benefit the crofters. Of course, only the very best would be accepted .

Edward Standen, a regular visitor to Shetland, bought many Shetland garments to sell in his shop in London. He and Arthur Anderson made tremendous efforts to bring Shetland knitted goods to the market notice of people in Britain.

Most articles were knitted without a pattern, just plain. Arthur knew that his friend Samuel Laing had visited the islands lately. On his return home his daughter had sent a beautiful Christening cap to baby Ogilvy, made in Lille thread – very delicate. It was much admired and talked about. A Shetland woman who saw it copied the pattern in a pair of mittens and from there the idea of garments in lace became popular in shawls and even stockings. Instead of using thread, the women used very fine spun wool. This wool was pulled or 'rooed' from the neck of the little Shetland sheep – it was very fine.

It was time also that the women were paid a lot more for their time, thought and effort put into their articles.

Arthur's father, Robert, being an Unst man, knew Mrs Elizabeth Edmondston of Buness who was an expert knitter. He would encourage his wife to write to her and several other ladies to send some of their first class articles to her so that she in turn could send them off to Arthur who was going to present them to Queen Victoria, in the hope of boosting the islands' knitting industry.

When the garments had been gathered together they were posted to London. Arthur was delighted as he and Mary Ann lovingly handled the exquisite woollens and admired the many patterns such as 'waves, shell, diamond, spider's web, cat's paw etc'.

When Arthur received permission from the Queen to present the garments she was so delighted she immediately ordered one dozen pairs of stockings. The bill she said was to be sent to her. The Duchess of Kent also received articles and was delighted with them.

Now that the most important person in the country had made a valuable purchase of the fine woollen garments, Arthur trusted that many of her subjects would do likewise, encouraging a struggling croft industry to begin in earnest.

Arthur also fought against the Corn Laws which threatened ruin to Shetlanders. With the rise in population, land was becoming scarce. Larger crofts were divided to make more smaller ones. Crofters were forced to grow all they needed in the way of potatoes, cabbage, oats and beremeal. The fowls gave eggs and meat, the cattle produced milk and meat, pigs for meat and sheep for wool and mutton. These animals also had to be hand-fed in the winter months when the weather was too severe to find food outside. Ponies provided the necessary transport for peats and people going long distances. Many a time the crops failed and the crofters starved. Fish was their staple diet. Those caught in the summer months were salted down for winter consumption, along with mutton and beef.

Crops of oats and bere were grown extensively. The oats grown in Shetland were of a hardy type, able to withstand the rigours of the harsh climate and to thrive in poor soil. The seeds were ground in small watermills for flour and the straw used for making kishies or baskets, also for thatching roofs and bedding for the beasts.

The animals on the islands are of a small breed and do not need much to feed on. They are out in all weathers, except the domestic ones which are often in the same cottage as the family or in an extension off the living quarters.

Many crofters were reluctant to improve their land as they might be evicted by the landlord on some paltry excuse. All their hard work would be wasted but be of great benefit to the person succeeding them.

The only means of opening up a new field or piece of ground was by the spade. Five or six women in a row digging with their Shetland spades kept in time as they dug, lifted and turned the soil, often to a song.

The small ponies were used to draw a home-made wooden plough and sometimes the women themselves pulled a harrow on the rough ground in order to smooth the surface of the soil.

Arthur well remembered the sparse times his parents suffered during years of famine. Only a person who had lived under these conditions could realise what it was like. Arthur Anderson was one of them.

Chapter 8

A Friend's Tragedy

"Dear Son," wrote Robert Anderson. "It saddens me to have to write to you this letter but it must be done. Our good friend, Rev John Turnbull was at Dunrossness, he told me, visiting the Rev David Thomson. His good wife, Wilhelmina took Barbara and John and her maid, Bessy, to visit a crofter, no doubt with food as this was Christmas week. It had snowed all night and was very cold and the loch in front of the house was frozen over.

"Wilhelmina and her party were returning to the manse and being later than expected they thought it would be safe to cross the loch. However, when they got halfway across the ice gave way and they all fell into the freezing water and were drowned. Two crofters passing at that moment saw the accident and jumped into a boat tied up at the loch side, breaking the ice as they went with their oars. They managed to drag the bodies out of the water and lay them on the bank. By this time a number of crofters had gathered. They made stretchers and carried the bodies up to the manse.

"They sent a rider post-haste to tell Rev Turnbull to come at once. One couple took the remaining nine children to their cottage so they would not see the dead being carried into the house.

"When the rider came to the manse at Dunrossness he knocked on the door and gave his message but did not tell the reason why.

"John thanked his host for his stay and left saying that he would call another time. All the way home, poor John's thoughts were racing. What could have happened?

"He was soon on his way past Levenwick, wondering all the time what tragedy had happened in his absence. He urged his horse on as he passed the Brig of Eigg then Sandwick and rode carefully past the cliffs at Cunningsburgh. He knew there was a bull kept in the park he had to cross so he dismounted, opened the gate and mounted the horse again and galloped to the next gate in safety. He passed the little cottages clustered on the hillside at Ocraquoy then down the hill into Quarff.

"It was getting dark now and he could not slacken pace but he had to go a little slower as they wound their way up the hill to the Peerie Loch and on past Brindister to Gulberwick. Turning off the path to Lerwick, he went west on the path leading to the Brig of Fitch. As he came to the crest of the hill and rode down past Herrislea, he noticed that there were no lights on in the manse windows. Had Wilhelmina forgotten to tell the maids to light the candles? He was not due home till next day but the windows were always lighted at night time for anyone passing. Of course, Teena could do nothing unless her mistress instructed her. It was the same with the men on the croft he reflected. John was educated and this put a terrible distance between him and the people. How he longed that he could speak to them and they respond to him in a natural way.

"Entering the yard, he quickly gave the reins to Robert to put the horse in the stable. 'Give him a good rub down', he said, 'he has travelled twenty-six miles and is exhausted'.

"John went to the front door and entered then fumbled for a candle lying on the hall table. Lighting it, he went to the kitchen but there was no sign of Teena. He went through all the rooms downstairs then rushed up the stairs. By this time he was really worried. He opened the spare or guest room door and to his horror, in the candle light, he saw Wilhelmina lying on the floor, still in her clothes and Barbara and John lying one each side of her. Bessy was in a corner by herself. He knelt on the floor beside his wife and felt her face. It was cold but beautiful as ever. He put a hand on each of the children's faces and they too were cold. What had happened? Could the messenger not have told him? He could not think – he felt numb.

"John bent forward and placed a kiss on Wilhelmina's forehead. He found himself quoting a verse of scripture that he had often used to comfort others, 'The Lord gave, the Lord has taken away, blessed be the name of the Lord'.

"With that he rose up and went to his study where he sat at his desk and wept. How long he was there he did not know. But where were the children? He got up and went to the stable to ask Robert who was just shutting the door.

" 'Tell me Robert, where are the children?'

" 'At Mistress Eva's cottage, sir. She and her husband took them in. It is a sad day for you sir'.

" 'Yes', answered John in a daze, 'I will go and fetch them. See that the fires are lit in all the bedrooms so they will be warm'.

"John left the Manse and went to the cottage to find the children and Teena finishing off a hot drink. When he saw the children he nearly gave way to his sorrow. But no, he must be brave for them.

" 'Well children', he said, 'you know your mother, Barbara and John are not with us now – or Bessy. We will have to be brave and help one another. Thank you very much for caring so kindly for the little ones in my absence', he said turning to the couple.

"When all the children were in bed that night John went to his study.

"A sudden thought struck him, it was Thursday and he would have to preach a sermon on Sunday. But how could he? But he would have to as there was not time to get anyone else.

"The following morning he told Teena to have the children all ready and come to his study before breakfast. When the children were all assembled John looked at each one. Nine of them.

" 'Teena, stay in the room a minute please.'

" 'Elizabeth, as the oldest daughter, you will take the place of your mother and look after the children. They will', he looked at each of the children again, 'obey you as they did their dear mother. Right?' he asked.

" 'Yes, sir', they all whispered.

" 'Teena, you will look after the household as before and take your orders from Elizabeth. Understood?'

" 'Yes, Sir.'

" 'You may all come in for breakfast now', said father, leading the way to the dining-room.

"Many wondered if there would be a service on the Sunday but felt it best to go in case. The poor man rose to the occasion as only he could, taking his text from Ezekiel 24 v.18. 'So I spake unto the people in the morning and at even my wife died and I did in the morning what I was commanded'.

"Fancy that. I will write again, Father."

When Arthur read the letter he was devastated. Wilhelmina, the kind generous wife of his beloved tutor – gone, and little Barbara and John too. How could anyone sympathise with such a loss? Knowing John Turnbull, Arthur knew he would be a tower of strength to his family. They had been married for twenty-seven years and had eleven children. They had entertained many notable people and Wilhelmina was a perfect hostess.

Among their distinguished guests was H.R.H. the Duke of Edinburgh. Once while John was visiting Leith and Granton he was welcomed onboard the lighthouse ship by Sir Walter Scott. As the ship was leaving for Shetland, John travelled onboard with his host. Sir Walter was invited to say at the manse in Tingwall and enjoyed his visit immensely. John was able to supply much information about Shetland for 'The Pirate', a book Sir Walter was writing. On Sunday he accompanied the family to church. He was later heard to say that the Rev John Turnbull looked after his flock, not only spiritually but materially as well, in gifts of meal and vegetables grown in his garden. Sir Walter said the 'glebe' was the best he had seen in Shetland.

Arthur read a post-script to the letter:

"Before I close, may I add that Balfour Spence's son, James Ross has become Dutch consul instead of his father. He is also a shipping agent, merchant and broker and his firm is situated at Commercial Street above Sinclair's Beach. He is also vice-consul for the Hanseatic Republic. He sells clogs and hosiery too and I often see medicines in the window."

Arthur turned round as he heard the door open and his wife come in . "Sit down my dear," he said.

"Why, whatever is the matter? You look ill."

"Read this," was all Arthur could say.

Mary Ann read the letter pausing occasionally to wipe the tears from her eyes.

"I can hardly believe it," she whispered, "Wilhelmina, Barbara and John all gone, also little Bessy, so young and helpful. But isn't that typical of John to quote that lovely verse. He has such a peace in his heart but he must feel bereft."

"I shall write him today," said Arthur "and send him our condolences."

Chapter 9

The Birth of P&O

"Read this," said Brodie Willcox to Arthur Anderson as he sat at his desk one morning two years after the loss of the *Don Juan*, "they still have confidence in us."

Arthur studied the letter in his hand. It was from the Admiralty inviting the company to consider drawing up a scheme enabling the company to extend their journey from Gibraltar through the Mediterranean to Egypt and the port of Alexandria, some 2,000 miles distance. The suggestions submitted were successful and in 1840 the company won the contract.

Always looking ahead, Anderson suggested to Willcox that they might as well think of taking the mails to India and offer for that contract at the same time! No doubt Willcox was baffled as to how they could get mails to India when they arrived at Alexandria! Arthur would assure his partner that they had not been beaten yet and once a Shetlander got an idea into his head it usually materialised.

"But," Arthur would continue, "once we have surmounted the difficulty of getting to India, we can go on from there to Penang, Singapore, China and …"

"Oh come on Anderson, one place at a time," said Willcox , "let's think of Alexandria and the ships we need for that run first."

"And, eventually," persisted the dreamer, with a faraway look in his eyes, "to Australia and New Zealand. Why not? Remember how we started with the little sloop? We now have a whole fleet of ships but we need to keep expanding. We have faith that if we provide the facilities then trade will follow. Our passengers are content because we provide the best for their comfort, leisure and cuisine."

"Our staff are happy and we pay them adequately and they get along well with one another. If we are going to extend our routes to the Orient we would need to add that name to the company's heading – don't you think," asked Arthur smiling.

"Whoever said we were going to the Orient," queried a now worried Willcox, "we haven't reached Egypt yet."

"Look ahead," was the answer. "And I think we should add another partner to our new company. What do you say?"

"I agree wholeheartedly," Willcox breathed, glad that someone else would be able to share his anxieties.

"What about Francis Carleton?" He has been a tower of strength to us lately."

"None better," agreed Willcox. "What will we call the new company?

"I think the Peninsular and Oriental Steam Navigation Company would be fine," answered a satisfied Anderson.

"Rather a mouthful," laughed Brodie.

"Well, why not call it P&O?"

"That sounds better. Shall I ring for Carleton to come in?"

"Certainly. Come in Carleton. We are to launch another company and would like you to be one of the directors. It will be called "The Peninsular and Oriental Steam Navigation Company" which we have shortened to P&O. What do you think?"

"I should be honoured to become one of the directors," answered Carleton.

And so P&O was born.

"Willcox," said Anderson as the three directors signed the newly drawn-up charter, "you will preside over the company headquarters here in London. I shall travel to the various ports of call to make arrangements for developments in the said quarters. Carleton, you can begin by commissioning a couple of ships for our latest venture. Southampton to India. The ships will need to be larger than any we already have to combat the rough seas around the Cape of Good Hope and the monsoons in the Indian Ocean. It does seem ridiculous to me to have ships travelling round South Africa when we could go as the crow flies across the Suez. It's only 150 miles of desert."

"I think I'll see about the ships," said Carleton, "at least they are not fantasy!"

For nights Arthur lay awake, waking his wife every hour or so to tell her of the new scheme he had planned.

"But how can you think of that as a possibility?" she asked – "even Napoleon tried it but failed to even get it started."

"But we would be different," persisted the excited Arthur, "I know a Frenchman who could survey the area then he could give us an idea of what could be achieved. I shall go and visit him when the next mail packet goes to Portugal." Arthur slept that night peacefully as he had now made up his mind to visit France and thus conquer the situation.

Once the Frenchman had pronounced the idea of constructing a canal between the Mediterranean and the Red Sea, as feasible, Arthur immediately got in touch with the Foreign Secretary, Lord Palmerston, and urged him to persuade the government to build the canal. Lord Palmerston's pleas failed to interest the government and the project was dropped, much to Arthur's dismay and disbelief.

In the meantime, he set off on one of the mail boats to Alexandria. He could visualise a train of camels carrying goods and coal to the Red Sea. What was one hundred and fifty miles on land? The mails would be safer than on sea.

Chapter 10

Suez Canal

Anderson gained an audience with the Pasha of Egypt, Mohamet Ali. When told of the proposed journey across the desert, the Pasha promised to send guards to accompany the fleet across the Suez to protect them from raiders. The next thing was to organise transport for passengers for which Anderson obtained horse-drawn carriages. He ordered four thousand camels to carry freight. Places of rest for the passengers were organised as well as food and water.

The most difficult part of the operation was to supply the ships steaming between the Red Sea and India with coal. Here again, his imagination came to the rescue. He would send coal from Britain. Some undertaking! Sailing ships would off-load coal at designated ports on the Red Sea and in India to bunker the steamers.

As most of the coal came from South Wales and the P&O ships left from Southampton, Arthur formed a company called the Union Steam Ship Company. He had ships built ships for the job and they were very successful. He soon had quite a fleet of ships under the Union name and later obtained a contract to take coal to Brazil and South Africa.

One morning, Arthur Anderson called Commander Engledue into his office.

"Congratulations," he greeted his colleague, "you are now superintendent of the P&O fleet. You have done well Engledue. I knew you could make it."

"Thank you, sir."

"I shall be leaving shortly for Egypt and I wish you to come with me. I need your advice on what type of ship should be built for use on the canal between Alexandria and Cairo. At the moment the only transport are the river dhows. They are much too small for our requirements. I am anxious to have a proper boat for the journey and am sure you will be able to come up with an idea that will be suitable. Now that we have the go ahead to cross the desert to Suez, we will need to provide our own transport for the passengers to Cairo first."

"There is so much to think off and plan that I would appreciate it if you accompanied me. We shall travel on the next boat to Alexandria."

When the pair arrived at Alexandria they took a dhow up the forty-eight mile long canal to Cairo. It took hours and was uncomfortable. Passengers with bags of goods and animals covered in fleas all travelled together and the heat too was overpowering with no shade.

"We shall obviously have to have a covered boat to begin with," said Anderson mopping the sweat from his face. A small steam boat would be ideal, it would shorten the time spent travelling and be clean."

"I would say a small tug," suggested Engledue, "the only thing is we would not have room for passengers, food and baggage. It cannot be a large boat because there is no depth to the canal."

"What about a couple of barges?" asked Arthur.

"Good idea, then the tug could pull them with the foodstuffs and baggage and have two more barges for the passengers. By the way, I noticed that the river is a different level from the canal. Goods are removed from the dhow on the river and carried to the next dhow on the canal to the higher level."

"No bother," smiled Anderson, "we'll build a lock to raise or lower the water then the boats can go through."

"The next headache is 150 miles of desert," pondered Engledue, "till we reach Suez and the Red Sea. How do you expect to achieve that, Sir?"

"It's all thought out," answered Anderson confidently, "we shall order horse-drawn buses for the passengers and donkeys for their luggage. It will take 18 hours, plus 12 for rest and refreshment. We shall use camels for the coal"

"Coal?" queried the mystified man.

"Yes, there is no coal here and when the people get to Suez the boats will have to be loaded with coal, so I have thought it all out. We shall have bunkers at Alexandria and Cairo for the tug and Suez for the ships coming up the Red Sea. There will be bunkers at Aden for the ships going to Calcutta. I wish we could get permission to dock at Bombay."

"But, but ….," began the bewildered man.

"We need coal," said Arthur patiently, "so it must be brought from Wales. I have ordered ships to be built, the Union Castle Line, to take coal to ports on the south coast where it will be shipped to Alexandria, then up to Suez by camel. It would be so much easier to build a canal all the way, but time will tell."

"Sir, we will need piers to be built at the different stopping places and warehouses for the goods to be stored till they are needed."

"I have thought of all that," stated a satisfied organiser, "we shall build resthouses along the route for sleeping and eating and, of course, changing the horses and donkeys and picking up more food for the journey."

"How are you going to keep food fresh in the heat? There will be meat and eggs, etc. ...."

"Farms will be provided for keeping animals for milk, eggs, butter and bacon and, of course, water will not be available so plenty stocks of wine, beer and water will be brought out. The ships will also have to carry live animals and have farmers to look after them."

Engledue rubbed his forehead. "Is the desert safe?" asked the worried man.

"Oh, quite safe. I spoke to the Pasha and he is making sure we will be accompanied by a guard. He seems quite taken with the idea. I suggested he should run a railway track between Cairo and Suez but I do not think he will entertain the idea yet. He is in favour of a canal though," added Arthur smiling.

"The Admiralty are sending an officer to guard the mails on the overland route till we reach Suez. I have ordered two ships to collect us at Suez and take us to Calcutta, the *Hindustan* and the *Bentinck*, wooden paddle steamers, with two funnels and three masts. They are quite magnificent and will be luxurious compared to the desert crossing. It will cut off a long journey round the Cape and the bad seas there. The monsoons might upset a bit but I have every confidence in the two ships, they will ride out any storm."

"I am amazed at the work and thought you have put into this project, sir, I just trust everything will go according to plan."

"Thank you, Engledue, now we can go home again and put the plans into action. We have to persevere if we want to get on you know."

Arriving back at the offices of P&O Anderson went in to see Willcox who was anxiously awaiting news of the trip.

"Excellent," he shouted as he heard of the plans, "but I might have known it would succeed if you had anything to do with it!"

"I must get down to ordering the animals to carry our luggage," mumbled Arthur as he left Willcox, "let me see now, four hundred and fifty horses, umpteen donkeys and about two thousand five hundred camels, I reckon would take care of the journeys."

Having sorted this problem out, Arthur now faced the fact that a company already ran luxurious ships from India to Britain. But they were sailing ships and took a year to do the round voyage – starting from Bombay on the West Coast.

The directors of P&O wrote to the East India Company asking if they could also sail from Bombay in the government mail boats. They were refused. Instead, they were given the option of sailing to and from Calcutta which meant a long voyage round the south of India and all the way up the east coast again. However, it was either that or nothing.

As the P&O company grew and extended its journeys to many British ports of call, it was felt that a new court of directors should be set up with Willcox and Anderson as joint managing directors.

The company received its Royal Charter in December, 1840. Having promised to extend their service to India the company fulfiled that undertaking in September 1842 when the *Hindustan* sailed for Calcutta. The *Bentinck* followed later. These two ships were to ply between the Red Sea and India.

Still forging ahead, Arthur mentioned the prospect of the Orient trips becoming a reality. The other directors of the company by now realised that what Anderson hinted at usually came to pass, so they agreed to sign a contract to take the mails as far as Penang, Singapore and China.

Now there was no holding Anderson back and in 1852 the contract was extended to Australia and New Zealand.

Chapter 11

News from 'Home'

Robert Anderson continued to keep his son informed of events in Shetland. He was sad to hear of the loss of the *Don Juan* but thankful that there was no loss of life. Having seven children from his second marriage, he enjoyed telling Arthur of their progress. He was also delighted to hear the news each time his son wrote of further commitments of the P&O line.

Sometimes he would think of the little boy going to school in Lerwick admiring the huge sailing boats in the harbour, or the beach-boy scraping the ling at the seashore or the willing youngster, so eager to help, plodding his way up the peat hill with Bess. He remembered the time he lifted the sleeping boy off his chair at the bedroom table and put him in his bed, still sound asleep.

Robert found himself reminiscing many a time. He was getting older now, nearly 84. He could hardly keep up with his son's activities – Portugal, Spain, Egypt and now India. He liked the shortened version of the company name – P&O.

In his last letter, Arthur had mentioned pleasure cruises in the Mediterranean. What would the boy think of next? It was certainly a far cry from the little boat in which he rowed Thomas Bolt back and fore to Bressay. Changed days indeed.

Robert sat back in the old Shetland chair at the open fireside. His wife was baking bannocks on the grid-iron. The kettle was singing on the crook hanging from the chimney. It was all so peaceful. The old man shut his eyes.

"Here's your tea, Robert," said his wife, "and a fresh baked bannock with homemade butter I churned this day. Robert, wake up." There was no reply. Robert had passed away peacefully at his own fireside.

Rev John Turnbull on his way in to Lerwick called along Da Böd of Gremista as he usually did on his way into town. He was very upset to find Robert gone but was a great help to his wife. He also undertook to write Arthur and Mary Ann to tell them the sad news.

Rev Turnbull left Gremista that day a sad man but glad to have been of help and able to give comfort to the family he had grown to love. Little was he to know that before that year was to end he too would lose a loved one.

His son, Robert, was a merchant in Scalloway. He had offered to take a man to Reawick in his sailing boat but it capsized and they were drowned.

John's oldest daughter, Elizabeth, who was married to Rev William Peterson, was on her way to Australia when the ship was wrecked and she died as a result. Further tragedy struck the family two years later when John's eldest son, William, who was an army doctor, died at sea. Now he only had his youngest daughter left, Grace, who after the death of her father went to Lerwick to live in the Old Manse.

After Robert Anderson died, Arthur was very upset as he had gained a lot of local news from his letters. However, Rev Turnbull had also kept up a correspondence with his former pupil at times, and now he wrote regularly for which Arthur was very grateful.

"I was passing the end of Sinclair's Beach today," wrote John, "when Gibbie Willliamson, the bellman, went past. He was shouting about getting gas lights for Lerwick houses and lighting for the street at night. What a boon that would be to the folks in town. It is hard to study by candlelight but when that is the only means it has to suffice. We will just have to be content with candles in the country though.

"There are to be over twenty lamps along the street, also some in the lanes and courts. The gas company started here about four years ago and built a pier to help transport their materials. The pier is used by small sloops arriving with coal. A plank of wood is put from the boat to the pier and sometimes it is the women who carry the coal in their kishies to the shore. It is a dirty job but I suppose it will bring in some much needed money to some of them.

The meal roads are a great success as they need the men to work to make the roads and being paid in meal keeps the families alive. The paths get very sodden in winter and are a danger to all who have to travel.

"William and Ursula Irvine have bought the old house at the South End, originally Sand's or Bain's Court. Many a cup of tea you and I had there. I remember entertaining Sir Walter Scott there too. I believe Irvine is changing the name to 'Irvinesgord'. Pity, but time moves on and I suppose we have to accept change at times. Irvine has a shop at the foot of Norna's Court.

"Lerwick decided to celebrate the victory of the Crimean War and Simon Milne, sergeant at the fort, fired several of the guns. It was not a good idea as the repercussions broke many windows in the nearby houses.

"George Laurence has come back to Lerwick as a qualified plumber – much needed. He had helped to instal gas and put in most of the fittings. He runs a general grocery business at the Stone Block just north of Sinclair's

Beach. He has taken over the auctioneers' business that James Bain ran as he is retiring. John also has started a drapers shop at the foot of Queens Lane. Busy man.

"I must remember to collect my watch from Robert Davidson. I can still see the proud look on your face as you showed me the watch your parents had bought for you from Robert.

"I was very sad about Kirstie Cadell and her three peerie bairns. She was evicted from her house and not given any help financially. Friends helped but Kirstie died in the Tolbooth. The Poor Inspector was blamed and he left his job. What a terrible thing in this day and age.

"I was along Andrew Nicolson's shop today asking about sailing times. His son is very fond of music and should one day be quite famous. He also makes up poems and songs.

"You'll remember Peter Laurenson at Gremista Farm? I hear he is thinking of emigrating to America. Scott, his brother, has been there for some years now. They were good neighbours to your folks at Da Böd.

"A contemporary of Peter's was Robert 'Snuddie'. He had a sister Janny Keetie and they lived in Hangcliffe Lane. Your father used to get him to slaughter his sheep to salt down for winter. Robbie was a character, really up to all kinds of mischief when young. He was an expert at climbing cliffs to get at the bird's eggs. He would board ships and climb the rigging when no-one was watching. He used to cheat the Dutchmen by giving them old buttons instead of change.

"John."

Chapter 12

Rigours of an MP

It was a cold morning, 12th February, 1828 in the town of Lerwick, that a midwife delivered a lovely baby boy.

"Mrs Bain," she said to his mother, "you have a son. What will you call him?"

"His name will be George," was the reply, "a chum for his nine older brothers."

George's parents were James and Andrina Bain. James was an auctioneer. The little boy proved to be a lively youngster and at the age of five attended the Heddell's School. He was a brilliant scholar and always eager to learn. He became an adept student.

He enrolled at the college Arthur Anderson had built in London for young recruits joining the navy. He studied and passed all his exams and in 1844 became a cadet and joined the P&O company.

Arthur was extremely pleased with the young lad's progress and followed his achievements closely. When it came time for Arthur to go to Shetland to canvas for names for his position as MP who could he choose better to sail his yacht to the islands than George Bain? Not only was it advantageous to Anderson to have someone who knew the seas around Shetland and Orkney as well but it was an opportunity for George to visit his relatives also.

When the time came for Arthur to sail north to Shetland to canvas for his role as MP he asked Commander Bain (P&O title instead of Captain) to sail his yacht. George was delighted to oblige and felt very honoured to sail the Thule with her owner onboard.

Meanwhile at Arthur's home in Surrey, Mary handed him a letter. It was from an old friend, Dr James Scott.

"I wonder what James thinks of my suggestion he accompanies me to the isles," mused Arthur, "Oh dear, he says he has been an invalid in bed for a period but hopes shortly to be better and able to come with me so we can canvas the islands together. Isn't that fantastic? A real friend. He says we are to pick him up at Leith as we travel north."

"Is it wise for him to be travelling?," asked MaryAnn.

"My dear, he says nothing will stop him coming now, he loves a bit of adventure. We will sail on the *Thule* from London. She will be a real novelty in the islands and very handy taking round the voes and isles. We will stop at each one we come to and hire ponies to take us to the cottages. I am so looking forward to this trip!"

"It is a pity your father did not live to see this day," said Mary Ann.

"Yes, he would have helped all he could. However, life has to go on and as we are quite comfortably off we can help others to experience the good things of life."

"You are always thinking of others Arthur. You really are a remarkable person." Mary hugged her husband.

"But I have you to help me," said Arthur returning her embrace. "We shall stay at Walter Sinclair's Queens Hotel in Lerwick so you can always write me there if there are any messages."

"It was sad last time you were abroad and dear John died. There was no way of getting word to you till you arrived back at Gibraltar."

"It will be fine to see Cathrine and the seven children. I am glad father married again after mother died and had a family as he was always very fond of children. It will be more convenient if James and I stay together at the hotel then we can arrange each evening where we will travel to the next day."

Dr Scott was about seven years senior to Arthur. A distinguished naval surgeon he had served under Lord Nelson and in several other ships before being shipwrecked in the St. Lawrence River while serving on the *Banterer*. This did not deter him from his career and after being with another four ships, he left the sea.

In 1815 he graduated from the University of Paris. He became lecturer at the Royal Naval Hospital at Haslar in 1826 and after eight years he resigned his post and went to live in Portsmouth. The honorary rank of Deputy Inspector of Hospitals and Fleets was conferred on him in 1846.

When the *Thule* arrived in Leith, Dr Scott was there to greet her. Her persuaded his wife, Kathrine, to come onboard and enjoy a tour of the ship. Afterwards, James accompanied her to the waiting gig where he waved her goodbye as she was driven back to their home in Musselburgh.

Arthur was up very early on the morning the *Thule* approached Sumburgh Head. He and George marvelled at the older sailing ships and how they had battled with the elements while under sail alone. *Thule* was one of the first steam ships but she still retained her sails.

It was exciting approaching Lerwick Harbour in the early morning with the sun rising over Bressay and bathing the little town in a golden glow. "It's good to be home again," said Arthur as he breathed in the fresh, salty sea air.

"Yes," replied George, "nowhere has quite the same air about it as Shetland and to a Shetlander it is always 'home'."

As the boat lay at anchor in the familiar harbour, a small rowing boat approached them from the town. John Ratter was the oarsman. He was employed by the North of Scotland and Orkney and Shetland Steam Navigation Company to ferry passengers from the ships to the beach. Having had word that the *Thule* was arriving, John had taken more care than usual to look smart as he was to be rowing one of the P&O directors to the town and with him would be Commander Bain and Dr Scott. A couple of leather boxes were lowered into the boat then Arthur and James climbed down the rope ladder and took their seats in the flit-boat.

Landing at Sinclair's Beach, Arthur and James employed a couple of boys with ponies to carry their boxes to Walter Sinclair's hotel, between Scotshall Court and the Half Nepkin. The hotel was warm and comfortable and the gentlemen were soon settled in their rooms. A beautiful meal was served, including Shetland lamb which they enjoyed. The rest of the day and evening was spent in arranging for the following days trips to the country districts.

"I think we will call along 14 Commercial Street and see Andrew McBeth about hiring a gig on the days we will not be sailing," said Arthur . "Then I must call along Robert Davidson and see how he is. I got my first watch from him. See, here it is, still going as accurately as when I got it from father the day I sailed south. I must ask Robert if he is still in charge of the Parish clock. He felt very honoured to get that job."

As the two men walked along the street, someone shouted "Andrew, James, it's good to see you both again. How are you? I knew Arthur was coming up but didn't realise you would be with him also James."

"I am very fortunate to have my friend and surgeon onboard," laughed Arthur, "but see who is joining us now! Our friend George, or should I say, Commander Bain?"

"Good day," said John Turnbull as he shook hands with the captain, "it's good to meet you all together, come to Elizabeth Walker's at 89 and have a coffee with me before you start the day's journey."

As they settled down to wait for their coffee, John said to Arthur "you have done well and I trust you will get the MP's job for Orkney and Shetland."

"Thank you," said Arthur, "I owe a lot to you for the beginning of my education and to Thomas Bolt for his parting words to me to 'Do Weel and Persevere'. Thank you for writing to me so regularly since father died, it keeps me in touch with all that is going on."

Once coffee and the chat was over, Arthur, James and George left their host and going along the street James said, "I must get an umbrella, I forgot to take mine with me."

"You will not keep one up in the wind here," laughed Arthur. "I think old Willie Henderson still has his shop along here. Here is Margaret, his daughter, opening her shop, we'll ask if her father is still in business." Margaret assured the men that he certainly was and he would be glad to see them and have a speak. James bought his umbrella and as they left the shop they met John Turnbull coming along carrying a new saddle.

"I have just been along James Levack purchasing this saddle. It's a beauty. I ride a lot. He still lives at 3 Church Lane. We'll get together again and have a game of billiards at Walter's some time."

"I see Arthur Smith has retired," Arthur observed to James. "He used to have Candle House at Gardie Court. Many a candle we bought from him. I believe it was James Sinclair who installed the town's gas works. That is a great step forward."

"Yes," answered James, "all your studying had to be done by candlelight I believe. I was fortunate to be in London."

"Here are some of the posters I sent to Jimmy Johnson to distribute around the islands advertising the campaign for electors."

Arthur Anderson had been concerned about getting the mails safely to the Peninsula, now he felt the time had come to help improve the mail service to his native islands. In 1837, Arthur wrote to Her Majesty's Treasury explaining the situation and pleaded for a steamer packet to be sent to convey the mails to Shetland. Eventually, the government relented and a steam packet named the *Sovereign* sailed to the islands in April, 1838.

In regard to the repeal of the Corn Laws in 1846, Anderson prepared a petition to be presented to the House of Commons informing them of the conditions in Shetland. The inferiority of the soil to grown corn, bad weather causing loss of crops, not enough men for the fishing to pay for corn to be brought into the islands. Many of the able-bodied men were serving in the navy which left the women to do all the work on the croft, besides looking after their family and parents.

When Arthur stood for Parliament in 1847 his opponent was Fredrick Dundas. What hope had Arthur to win the election? Nothing daunted, he set about this task as he always did with a free mind and determined spirit.

Canvassing for an election in a town is hard work but easy compared to trudging over heather clad hills or riding on a small pony. However, the first morning in Lerwick, Arthur and James Scott went to 14 Commercial Street and spoke to Andrew McBeth about hiring his gig for visiting cottages in Sound, Gulberwick and Scalloway. They had to travel extensively by pony arriving at the various voes and hiring the ponies from the crofters there. On fine days the work was pleasant but thoroughly miserable on a wet or foggy day.

The men were amicably received by the lairds and merchants as they remembered how recently Arthur Anderson had helped repeal the Corn Laws.

Not everyone was friendly though. Arriving at one bay, the men rowed ashore from their yacht and went to the laird's house nearby. "Surely he will vote for you," said James encouragingly, "he looks prosperous enough."

"He may even give us something to eat," added Arthur, who was feeling quite tired and hungry.

James lifted the heavy knocker on the huge front door. It was opened by a servant who asked what their business was.

"We wish to speak to the laird," began James, "about signing a paper in support of Arthur Anderson who is a candidate in the coming election for Orkney and Shetland."

The pair heard a voice booming out from the inside, "I certainly shall not be supporting one of Thomas Bolt's flunkeys."

With that, the door was shut and the two men made their way to the waiting ponies, highly amused at the thought of the now wealthy man being called a 'flunkey'.

Not having seen a steam yacht before, many of the islanders were amazed when they first observed a ship coming steaming into the bay with no sails, yet going very fast and with smoke billowing out of its funnel.

Each evening, Arthur and James returned to either the yacht or Lerwick very tired but pleased at the reception of the people.

"We will travel as far as Tresta tomorrow," said Arthur, "and we can stay with George Johnson at the hotel. There are stables for the horses as it is a posting station for the mails where the horses will be changed so that fresh ones can carry on through Bixter. There is also a shop there."

"Good idea Arthur, then we can canvas Tresta and into Sandsound. We will take the boat other days when there is no hotel to say at and that will save having to come back to Lerwick each night."

"We shall need to buy some woollen garments to take home before we leave. I think Mary Ann would like a lace cardigan. What about Kathrine?"

"I think she would fancy a Fair Isle jumper," answered James, "as she always feels the chill. There is nothing like the Shetland wool for keeping the cold out. Better buy something for ourselves too."

Arthur Anderson kept in touch with George Bain and in 1852 they were again in Shetland. George's brother, Gilbert, home from business in Singapore, accompanied him on a visit to see their mother, Andrina Bain, who now lived at Lochend House of which she had the life rent.

Arthur was a frequent visitor to Lochend House and he often reminisced over the times he would row Thomas Bolt across the sound and come to the house for a welcome refreshment. One day Arthur took his niece, Elizabeth Johnson to visit and when she and George met they became friendly.

"I hear that Dr Loeterbagh has settled in Shetland," he told Andrina Bain. "I used to see him attending the men onboard the Dutch vessels but, being Dutch, I believe he had to study in Edinburgh before he could practice here. He is staying at Navy Cottage. We have seen many changes here through the years."

"We truly have," said Mrs Bain as she nodded her head.

"I believe George Laurenson is now auctioneer in place of your husband James."

"Yes, indeed," answered Andrina, "Jock Murray continued in the joinery business in Bain's Court till it was bought by William Irvine, father of John who is the artist. He changed the name to 'Irvinesgord' but I think most folks still call it Bain's Court. I hear you have been visiting the Skerries."

"I have, and there is a school established there now – also a teacher. The authorities have not got round to providing any education in the islands and there are so many youngsters eager to learn. I felt compelled to provide the necessary means for them."

By 1854, Willcox resigned as a managing director of P&O and four years later became chairman of the court of directors. Arthur Anderson was now managing director.

John Turnbull still kept Arthur up to date with all the happenings in Shetland. He said Lerwick was beginning to look like a modern town now with its gas lights on the street and in some of the homes. A very useful sawmill was functioning and handled by Alfred and Laurence Stove. They were fortunate to have their own MP, Fredrick Dundas, but missed Arthur as he had such a knowledge of the islands' requirements and the needs of the people.

Charles Duncan was an able man about town being procurator fiscal and chief magistrate; as well as Dutch and Belgian consul. He was also dealing with a scheme to see that the water supply is kept clean and sewage properly taken care of. He is a busy man and factors several of the estates in Shetland. He had bought the property known as Sinclair's Beach and improved road surfaces and generally tidied up the town. "Much need" wrote John Turnbull.

Chapter 13

A.E.I. – A Longing Fulfiled

As Arthur read the accounts in John Turnbull's letters of children running riot in Lerwick, he became quite upset to think there were not enough places for them to be taught in the parochial school. He thought of the advantage he had had as a young boy to attend the Rev Turnbull's school. It had laid the basis of his education. After leaving school, he had gone back to the beach to clean fish, then joined Thomas Bolt in his office at Heogan. After that it was a case of being self-taught. It had helped that he was keen to learn, whereas some children needed to be encouraged at every stage.

"It is admirable that some young people have started what they call 'The Lerwick Instruction Society'," said Arthur to his wife. "I think I shall send some money to help them along. What do you say my dear?"

"Certainly," answered Mary Ann who was all for supporting her husband, "it may benefit someone."

"What they need is a large school to accommodate all the children. You know Mary Ann, I have an idea. I shall write the Lerwick Literary and Scientific Society and see if they can tell me if there is any ground in Lerwick on which a school could be built."

After a few weeks a letter arrived from the Lerwick Literary and Scientific Society and Arthur opened it anxiously to see what news they had for him.

"Well, well, Mary Ann," he stated, "this is a letter from the Lerwick Literary and Scientific Society and they say there is no ground available on which to build a school and it would also prove to be too expensive to build one. I shall write back immediately and tell them if they can find some ground I shall pay for the building myself."

Arthur also told the society that the school would be large enough to take five hundred pupils and all children of parents of any Christian denomination would be welcome. The school would be large enough to accommodate secondary education and an academy also.

The answer which Arthur received in response to this letter appalled him.

"Mary Ann, just listen to this," he said, "the Lerwick Literary andScientific Society don't want to know about a school. It is alright for these fee-paying parents who can afford to educate their children to dismiss my offer, but it's those who cannot pay for their education that I'm worried about. They might have been our own."

Arthur Anderson was a wealthy man by this time but he was also a very generous, kind-hearted person. He and his wife had no children of their own but his mind often went back to the times when he attended Rev Turnbull's school and how upset he had been to have to leave and go back to work. He felt there must be many a child in Shetland still facing that terrible quandary and he determined to do something about it.

Bitterly disappointed by the response, Arthur decided to go north himself and find a desirable site. He contacted an architect in Aberdeen, William Smith, and asked him if he would accompany him to Lerwick to survey the site and draw up plans for a school.

Arthur was able to purchase a site on the south side of Lerwick from Dr W. Spank of Greenfield. The situation was known as Dr Spence's Park. Smith was told the school was to be to accommodate five hundred pupils with other rooms for community activities.

"Can you give me an idea of how much this project will cost?" asked Arthur. "There has been no response from the local people to help financially so I shall have to foot the bill myself." Smith estimated that the cost at £6,000.

On 20th November, 1861, Arthur wrote to the Lerwick Literary and Scientific Society and told them how much the building of the school was to cost and would it be possible for them to ask the local people to contribute something towards the maintenance of the school, such as paying for books, teachers and the general cost of running it.

"I wonder what the society thought of my letter," said Arthur to his wife as he opened their response over breakfast one morning. "Well, well, they think I am to be praised for erecting such a magnificent building but the community has no desire to help to pay for it or any further outlay connected with it. That's a bit mean, isn't it? I am not going to be put off by these people. Maybe the country folks would be more forthcoming if they thought their children were to be included as well. I shall get posters printed and distribute them to the local shops asking for help. I shall place one in the Bank. I shall add on the poster that accommodation will be provided for the country children to stay in Lerwick."

Arthur got in touch with a master joiner, John Hardie at 12 Commercial Street and asked if he would be willing to undertake the joinery work of the new school. John was willing to oblige. He contacted William Sinclair of 4

Albany Street and they worked together. They joined as partners later, becoming Messrs. Sinclair and Hardie.

When the building of the Anderson Educational Institute was completed it was a truly magnificent sight, built in Jacobean Baronial style. And Arthur was justly proud of his achievement.

The society set a day to declare the school open – 14th August, 1862. They invited seventy gentlemen, the elite of the county to attend – no ladies! A dinner was served in the main hall, over which Andrew Grierson of Quendale presided, and after the meal many toasts were drunk to various societies and individuals – including Arthur Anderson and his wife.

"After the proceedings were over," Arthur told his wife when he got home, "the whole company walked with me to the pier where I was to get the boat home. The band played all the way and I felt quite a celebrity being piped aboard. I know it was worth all the outlay we have had to make to be sure of the young folks education.

"As the boat passed the South Ness on her way out of the harbour, 'The Institute' as they all call it looked beautiful – so stately and proud – dominating a large portion of the hill in which it stands. A lot is owed to you, my dear, for the constant encouragement you have given me to persevere in getting it built and running."

"If it's not ships to the Far East, it's a school in Lerwick. I need not say to you to sit back and take it easy because I know you better than that! So what is your next project?"

"To pay three pounds to the roads authority in Lerwick for repairs to the paths we have used throughout the building of the Institute. I think we will just about manage that," laughed Arthur.

"What a disgrace," said Mary Ann with feeling, "after all you have done for the town. I know many will appreciate your work in years to come. We will just pay the bill and say nothing."

Chapter 14

The Widows' Homes

As Mary Ann sat one evening in her lovely home at Norwood Grove her mind travelled back to the last time she and her husband had visited Shetland. She had often visited the poorer homes in Lerwick where some of the beautiful, delicate lace shawls and Fair Isle garments had been knitted. Some seemed to be just hovels where one room would be occupied by a large family. In the country districts, the crofters would have a cow, sheep, a peat bank and the wife kept hens, so there was always something to eat. In Lerwick, the fishermen's wives depended on the money their husbands made to stay alive.

What happened when the money-earner became ill or died? Sometimes the widows got work in the big houses or a shop or even carting coals off the ships which supplied the gas-works. Usually, they were given a bucket-full to take home as a bonus. Any job was considered that would bring in enough to feed and clothe the family.

Mary Ann was very upset to see the poverty amongst the widows and their children. The women endeavoured to patch tears in their long black skirts or red petticoats and mend holes in the shawls which covered their heads. They wore cow-hide 'rivlins' or moccasins on their feet if they were fortunate enough to procure some leather. The children usually went barefoot or in the very cold weather they wound pieces of cloth round their feet.

Not much seemed to be done to help these unfortunate ones. Mary Ann loved these little children and would fain have cuddled them but she was never allowed near them as their mothers pulled them along the street away from 'the lady', probably thinking she despised them.

This woman who had so much to give had learned that Shetlanders are an intensely proud and independent race and they do not accept help readily.

"Arthur," said Mary Ann in a pensive mood, "you have done such a lot to help educate the children in Shetland, providing schools and equipment for them. Then there are the lighthouses for the safety of the ships and work for the men. Then you encouraged the women to sell their knitted goods outside of the islands. I was just thinking ...," she hesitated.

"Yes, my dear, what were you thinking about?" asked Arthur looking lovingly at his wife.

"There are so many women whose husbands have been drowned and are now dependent on their families who are barely able to feed themselves and pay for the rent and fuel. They are proud women and sell the things they have knitted but that cannot be enough to cover their costs. Do you think something could be done for the widows? Last time we were in Lerwick it upset me so much to see the women, and some quite young, looking so weary and dejected, trailing along the street with their little brood, not knowing where to find food. It broke my heart.

"Oh, Arthur, I know you have been so generous but I would love to see a place where these women and girls, so attractive in their gentle ways, could live and be happy."

"Well, my dear," answered her husband, "we certainly have the financial means to help them and as I have got the school building under way, that could be our next project, to do something for the widows." Now that you mention it, there is a flat piece of ground near the 'Institute', just above the banks. That would be an ideal situation. The windows would face the harbour and they would be away from the crowded lanes."

"Wonderful," smiled Mary Ann. She had already begun to hatch plans for the little cottages. "There would be a space large enough for each to have a chicken-run outside so they could sell the eggs. Maybe the field next to that could be used for growing vegetables. Oh, I am so excited about it all," she finished.

If Mary Ann was happy about the prospect of the homes she had no idea how grateful and pleased the occupants would be in the future.

"Here is your post, sir," said the maid, as she handed Arthur Anderson the mail on a silver salver.

"Thank you," said Arthur. Then turning to Mary Ann he said "here is the *Shetland Advertiser.* Well, well, do you remember Gibbie Wood and Ann from Muckle Roe? They went to Australia in '54. I see they have started a wholesale and retail grocers shop in Adelaide. They used to order things from Thomas Bolt."

"But Arthur," interrupted Mary Ann," there is a wedding invitation here from your niece, Elizabeth's folks, inviting us to the wedding of Elizabeth and George. Isn't that wonderful? They will make a lovely couple."

At that moment, a knock came to the door and the maid handed in a telegram. Arthur's face went white as he read it.

"Whatever is the matter?" asked Mary Ann.

"It's Brodie. He has been killed by a falling tree. I just can't believe it. Brodie gone. They want me to come at once."

"Of course," said a still dumfounded Mary Ann."

"Tell John to get the gig ready while I change into my mourning clothes."

"You'll find your frock coat hanging in the double wardrobe and your tall hat in the leather box above with your white gloves."

It took many days for the truth to dawn on Arthur that his partner and friend would no longer be there to be consulted. What a disaster, after a working partnership of forty years.

Next time Arthur visited Lerwick, he asked permission of the council to erect homes for the most needy of the widows in the town. His proposal was accepted but no financial backing offered. However, the homes started to go up above the 'Duke's Neb' and many a widow looked longingly at the individually placed accommodation.

"Next time you go to Lerwick, I shall come with you," declared Mary Ann, "and I'll see for myself how the buildings are progressing. I should love to see them occupied and be able to visit the ladies."

"Perhaps, but you have not been looking well lately," said her husband sympathetically. "I think you should visit the doctor."

"Oh, I'm fine, just not as able as I used to be."

Arthur looked lovingly at Mary Ann as she sat at the fireside. She was so pretty in her pale blue dress with it's high neck, puffed shoulders and long tiered skirt. She always looked so regal. Her hair was piled high on her head and caught with a diamante comb. He was worried about her. She never grumbled about being ill but he sensed she was not well.

It was not long after this that Mary Ann took to her bed, very ill and died. Arthur was distressed and, for a while, inconsolable. They had been married for so many years and had planned and consulted each other over many things.

When a new venture came into Arthur's thoughts, he would look up from his writing desk to the chair where Mary Ann usually sat beside the fire, only to find it vacant, her little sewing basket beside it and her slippers in the fireplace. He would not allow them to be moved.

Sitting with his head in his hands, he would contemplate the problem in question and now have to make up his own mind.

At length, he decided that Mary Ann would prefer him to go ahead with whatever plan he had chosen to carry out and feel that she was still behind him in all his decisions. In view of this, Arthur had the privilege of opening the Widows' Homes in Lerwick, a ceremony which his wife had so desperately wanted to witness. He put a plaque on the front of the building which reads:-

'These homes for widows
were erected by

Arthur Anderson Esquire
A native of Lerwick
Chairman of the
Peninsular and Oriental Steam Navigation Company
Member of Parliament for Orkney & Shetland 1847 – 1852
IN MEMORY OF HIS WIFE
"I WAS A STRANGER AND YE TOOK ME IN"

The year was 1864, just a year after Mary Ann had died.

Arthur Anderson was very pleased to hear that Mrs Bruce Mullay was to be appointed matron of the homes. She was the daughter of Robert Davidson, the watchmaker, and he knew her well and felt sure she would do well in the job chosen for her. She had had six children but only one survived, a daughter, who lived with her mother.

After commiserating with Arthur in a letter on the death of Mary Ann, John Turnbull went on to tell him of the death of Sinclair Thomson. "He settled at Spiggie and owned a shop where he sold gin and became involved in the smuggling trade. He managed, like yourself, to escape the press gang. He was a great fiddler and played at many of the functions held around that district. However, he felt that being the precentor at the church, he should live a more quiet life and he became a Christian. Donald Bain, from the North Isles, visited him and he was persuaded to get baptised in the Spiggie Loch. He gathered some members around him and started a Baptist Church at Spiggie. He preached all through Shetland, including Lerwick."

Chapter 15

Chairman of P&O

Arthur Anderson had been on a tight schedule. He was making arrangements for his departure to Suez when word came for him to attend the opening of the Widows' Homes. He rang the bell beside the fireplace and when the maid appeared at the door he asked her to fetch his coachman/handyman, John, and also to tell his housekeeper, Martha, to join him in the lounge.

"Come in John," he told the coachman, "I shall be leaving for Shetland next week, then in three weeks for Suez again. I would like you to put my large wooden trunk in the spare room for my trip to Suez. I believe you have a note of the usual items I take with me when travelling abroad, but this time may be a bit different, extras to add I mean. Water bottles, sandals and shorts, along with the usual jodhpurs, hunting hats and safari tunics."

"Martha, you will see to my clothes for Shetland and Suez. My dear wife always laid them out for me to inspect but I shall trust you to do that as you usually pack them anyway. No putting Shetland jumpers in my Eastern trunk or shorts in the Shetland luggage," he laughed.

"It's a mercy to see him more like himself again," observed John as he and Martha left the lounge. Martha arrived in the kitchen to tell cook of their master's departure.

"That means two lots of 'cabin' biscuits," sighed cook, "I don't know why he fancies them, they are so hard and tasteless."

"It's maybe because he likes to remember eating them when he was a cabin boy!" suggested Martha with a smile.

"Oh well, I better start on them now," said cook, "as he always takes them when he goes sailing."

"Sir," said John during the evening, "I have got the trunks down and some of the clothes ready. I see some buttons missing so will get Martha to sew them on. We do miss Mrs Anderson for so many things, sir," he finished with a quaver in his voice.

"Yes John," we all do but life must go on and I am sure Mrs Anderson would have desired us to carry on the good work."

"Yes sir," John said as he left the master in the best mood he had seen him in since the mistress' departure.

As well as opening the Widows' Homes, Arthur also had the pleasure of declaring the Lerwick Central Public School open. Another of his dreams come to fruition, just two years after presenting the Anderson Educational Institute to the students of Shetland.

Arthur was now seventy-three years old and yet his plans and boundless energy never diminished. With the death of his partner, Willcox, in 1862, he was now elected chairman of the P&O company. Surely this was his greatest achievement. He was very sad that his dear wife, Mary Ann, did not live to enjoy this supreme moment with him.

Arthur received a lovely letter of condolence from John Turnbull when Mary Ann died. He seemed to know just the right words of comfort and encouragement to write. It seemed incredible that it was now twenty-six years ago since Wilhelmina and the children were drowned. John did not often mention his wife but this time he referred to Wilhelmina as if she had been gone only a short while. Their deep love for one another still lingered on.

Now it was Arthur's joy to receive a wonderful letter from John of congratulation on his pupil reaching the magnificent position of chairman. John said he was very proud of the boy he had taught over sixty years ago and could well remember the disappointment on his anxious little face as he told his tutor he wished to follow in his footsteps but was hindered because his parents could not afford to let him be educated owing to the poor harvest and lack of money.

This had certainly changed and Arthur was now the benefactor.

John mentioned that of late he had not been well but it was probably due to the cold weather. "If anything happens to me" he wrote, "I have made arrangements for Grace, the only one of the family living now, to reside at the Old Manse, Lerwick."

The next year Arthur had a sculpture moulded to present to the pupils of the 'Institute', as they lovingly called it, a bust of himself bearing the wise and much quoted advice of his former employer, 'Dö well and persevere'. The plaque hangs to this day in the original part of the former building, not only as a reminder of its founder, but as good advice for all.

Not only had this practical man been thinking of the needs of the pupils in Shetland, but being a kind man he was anxious about the education of his employees' children. He had a school built for them in London, which could take nine hundred pupils. There was also a smaller college built for P&O officers.

Chapter 16

"He did well and persevered"

The Suez Canal was nearing completion. Arthur sat back in his armchair and thought of all the planning that had gone into this tremendous undertaking. Many were the times he had been persuaded to give up such a ridiculous project, but he had gone on to achieve what even the Napoleanic Government could not. He thought of the camels, hotels, slaves, barges, bunkers, the Atfeh, steamers, coal, horses, the shore excursions, animals for the farmyards. It was all too much for the now elderly man. He needed to rest not wrestle any more. He missed Mary Ann terribly.

A knock came to the door, he sat upright.

"Sir," said John, "there is a visitor to see you."

"Thank you," said Arthur, now fully recovered from his rest, "bring us a cup of tea and one of my favourite biscuits. I believe cook made some ready for me to taken on my next voyage to Suez.

"I am so looking forward to going to the opening of the canal," Arthur said to his guest, "it is surely twenty-three years since we started the operation. It seemed like a dream then but it is wonderful what can be achieved when one sets ones mind to it."

"Now we have made it possible for the mails to go through Suez to Calcutta, our next task will be to see that we can get the mails to Bombay but, until then, we shall use the *Hindustan* and *Bentinck* to take the mails by South India and up to Calcutta. We shall then be able to go to Penang, then China and fulfil the ultimate dream of taking the mail ships round the world. I trust I shall be spared to see that day."

Meanwhile, Arthur Anderson became frailer and in 1868 he gave up the fight for life itself. He had faithfully followed the motto given to him almost sixty years previously.

Not many people have done so much as Arthur Anderson to help and encourage young and older people, not only in his lifetime but for generations to come.

Arthur Anderson is no longer with us, neither is the busy Dutch fleet, the happy laughter of the bustling gutter girls, nor the Press Gang but Da Böd of Gremista still stands proudly at the head of Bressay Sound.

Appendix

It may interest readers to know that the Suez Canal was opened in 1869, the year after Arthur Anderson died.

From India, the P&O spread to Hong Kong, Singapore, Japan, Australia, New Zealand, Western America, Panama and, with the purchase of the Orient Line, the company circled the globe. Arthur Anderson's dream had been realised.

Arthur Anderson was often referred to as "Sir Arthur" but, unfortunately, was never knighted, although he certainly deserved to be.

It was not until 1971 that P&O took over the North of Scotland and Orkney and Shetland Steam Navigation Company Limited, now referred to as P&O Ferries.

When Arthur Anderson tentatively advertised sea cruises in his paper *Shetland Journal* in 1835 to fill up a space, little did he think that cruising would become one of the most lucrative enterprises of the company.

Besides cruise ships, some of the largest ever built, the company owns many other forms of shipping transport, such as bulk shipping, cargo shipping and ferries. Recently a demerger took place creating the P&O Group for transport and P&O Princess Cruises.

The total operating profit for half-year up to the end of June, 1999, was an amazing £260.4 million.

Operating profits for the cruises for that year brought in, approximately, £245 million.